GRAVE
EXPECTATIONS

Alice Bell grew up in South West England, in the sort of middle-of-nowhere where teenagers spend their weekends drinking Smirnoff Ice in a field that also has at least one horse in it. She is the deputy editor of Rock Paper Shotgun, a popular PC gaming website, and in 2019 she was named one of the 100 most influential women in the UK games industry. After spending several years in London, Alice now lives in Cork in Ireland. She has probably read more detective fiction and watched more episodes of *Midsomer Murders* than you.

GRAVE
EXPECTATIONS

ALICE BELL

CORVUS

First published in Great Britain in 2023 by Corvus,
an imprint of Atlantic Books Ltd.

This paperback edition published in 2023.

10 9 8 7 6 5 4 3 2 1

A CIP catalogue record for this book is available from the British Library.

Paperback ISBN: 978 1 83895 842 8
E-book ISBN: 978 1 83895 841 1

Printed in Great Britain

Corvus
An imprint of Atlantic Books Ltd
Ormond House
26–27 Boswell Street
London
WC1N 3JZ

www.atlantic-books.co.uk

MIX
Paper | Supporting
responsible forestry
FSC
www.fsc.org   FSC® C171272

For Colm. hello Colm! iluyu!

and for Jay
ave atque vale

The Wellington-Forge Family Tree

Annotated Edition provided by Alex, the cool one

Nana Forge — m — Pappa Forge

(née Heal)

11/10 great-grandmother ever,
does not mind you smoking
weed in front of her

Didn't know him but
everyone says he was cool,
and he married Nana so
must have had good taste

Clementine Wellington-Forge ——— m ——

(née Forge)

Granny is a good cook but
tbh she has some bad vibes,
and she definitely does mind
you smoking weed

Figgy Wellington-Forge

Auntie F basically lives on
Harrods wallpaper swatches
and invites to prosecco
brunch in SoHo

Basher Wellington-Forge

Best uncle. Terrible hair.
Lets me live with him, which
is cool. Needs to loosen
up though.

Montgomery Wellington-Forge — m — Tuppence Wellington-Forge

(née Taylor)

He's my dad and even I can
see he's pretty fucked up. Even
for a London lawyer.

I wish mum believed she
deserves to be happy

Alex Wellington-Forge

Cooler, smarter, better looking
than you. The great hope for the
future. The one and only.

Hugh Wellington-Forge
(née Wellington)

Gun to my head I think the only thing I know about grandad is that likes brie and rugby

Tristan Wellington-Forge

Cruel thing to say about your own uncle but T is basically a standard embarrassing manchild

PART I

You think you will die, but you just keep living, day after day after terrible day.

Purported to be Charles Dickens in *Great Expectations* but actually manufactured by the internet

1

A Dead Girl

The train was two carriages long in its entirety, with rattling single-glazed windows, and it wound its way contentedly along the country line at whatever speed it felt like. It stopped at every tumbledown station it passed through, and this one was so small – a half-length platform of pebble-dashed concrete, covered in ivy at one end and collapsing at the other – that Claire almost didn't realize it was her stop. In the end it was Sophie who roused her from staring, unseeing, out of the window.

'Hey,' she said, waving a hand in front of Claire's face. 'I think this is it.'

'Oh, shit!'

Claire grabbed the bags and clattered out onto the platform just as the engine revved up once more. They turned and watched the train chunter off into the gathering darkness, then took stock. The letters on the sign were starting to peel off, but this was Wilbourne Major all right.

'*Ohmigod*,' Soph commented, as Claire shrugged on her coat. 'This place really is in the middle of nowhere.'

Claire turned round to look at her. Soph was in her usual bright turquoise velour tracksuit – Claire had almost forgotten what she looked like in anything else – the matching jacket and bottoms separated by a sliver of almost luminous midriff. Her chestnut curls were swept back into a high ponytail, and she had a few sparkly mini hair-claws in the shape of butterflies decorating the sides of her head. In fact it looked as if a giant butterfly had landed in the October gloom. Claire was struck, as she was more and more now that she was entering her thirties, by the strong protective urge she felt towards Sophie.

'Aren't we getting picked up? Where the *fuck* is the car?' Soph swore a lot – like, a lot a lot.

'Dunno.' Claire checked her phone. 'I haven't got any signal, of course. Figgy said she'd be here, though.'

'Let's go this way...' Sophie walked off the platform and through the hedge behind it. It turned out that the car park joined almost directly onto the platform, and there was indeed a car waiting on the far side of it. It was a very shiny black Audi.

'*Oof*,' said Sophie, as they walked towards it. 'How rich are they, again? Maybe this weekend won't be a total write-off.'

'I know, right?'

'Didn't you say everyone who has an Audi is a dick, though?'

'Yeah, they totally are. If you ever see someone driving like an arsehole, it's, like, always an Audi.'

'Isn't that like saying everyone who's rich is an arsehole?'

'I'm comfortable with that generalization,' Claire replied, picking at the loose threads in her coat. 'But shh. That's Figgy.'

'Sure, don't want to offend your rich arsehole friend. LOL.' Sophie pronounced it *el oh el*.

Figgy Wellington-Forge opened the driver's door and unfolded from the car like a sexy deckchair. She was very tall and was wearing a blue-and-white striped, figure-hugging woollen one-piece, as if she was off to an Alpine après-ski and not standing in mizzling rain in an English car park. She seemed exactly the same as she had been back in her university days with Claire.

'*Dah*-ling!' she cried, striding forward and bestowing Claire with four (four!) air-kisses. 'So good to see you.' Figgy was one of those people who stretched their vowels to breaking point, so what she actually said was: 'Seeeeeooo good to seeeyeeew!'

Claire slung the battered rucksack and holdall into the back seat, and Soph slid silently in after them. She sat in the middle because she liked to see the road. Claire sat in the front and then leaned back to fuss with the position of her rucksack, as a pretext to shoot Sophie a warning glance.

'Right!' Figgy exclaimed brightly. 'If we get a bit of a wiggle on, we should get to the house in good time for dinner. Mummy is doing shepherd's pie.'

Claire considered this. She'd had worse Friday nights than someone's mum making her shepherd's pie. It was getting truly dark now. When Claire looked in the rear-view mirror all she saw was the occasional oncoming headlight sparkling off Soph's lip gloss and her wide, dark eyes. Like most teenagers, Sophie's emotions passed across her face as quickly and obviously as clouds in front of the sun, but sometimes she switched off entirely and became totally impassive. It was quite scary.

Figgy shivered and put the heaters on full blast, then broke the silence that Claire suddenly realized had gone on for some time. 'So! How was your journey? God. It. Is. A. *Nightmare* getting down here, isn't it?'

Claire opened her mouth to agree – the trip from London had in fact taken the entire afternoon and a good portion of the evening – but Figgy didn't wait for an answer. She carried on chatting almost non-stop, while driving with the speed and abandon of someone who thinks they are a very good driver.

The car barrelled through the village of Wilbourne Major along back roads to Wilbourne Duces (an even smaller village that seemed more like a collection of houses around a pub and a postbox), and out into narrow lanes that twisted through fields. Claire found an opening eventually.

'Who's going to be here for the weekend, then? If you don't mind me asking,' she said.

'*Well*,' replied Figgy, intermittently taking her hands off the wheel to count off on her fingers, 'it's going to be almost all the family. There's Nana, obviously. She'll be hard to miss, she's the old lady in the wheelchair. Eighty-four on Sunday! Then there's Mummy and Daddy – Clementine and Hugh to you, I suppose. My sister-in-law Tuppence is here, too. She's married to my oldest bro, and brought their kid Alex along. Oh, and Basher's here, of course. He's the middle brother and he used to be a proper police detective, but he *totally* quit after the party last year. Bit of a sore spot with the 'rents, so maybe don't ask about it. Actually a huge sore spot. Massive drama.'

'Sorry, did you say "Basher"?'

'Ye-e-e-s! Sebastian, really, but nobody calls him that. I'm sure you met him. He came to a party at halls once.' Claire vaguely remembered a grave, blond young man with grey eyes eating all the Chilli Heatwave Doritos at a weekend pre-game before what was definitely not a pub crawl for Figgy's birthday (because pub crawls were unsanctioned by the uni, ever since a first-year chem student got alcohol poisoning).

'That's a load of people,' said Soph, who always kept track better than Claire. She often had to give Claire name prompts. 'Especially if more are turning up for the main party tomorrow.'

'It sounds like heaps, but it's actually less than last year,' said Figgy. 'Is it a problem?'

'Nah,' said Claire. 'I've, um, had bigger groups.' This was in fact untrue, but there was no reason to tell the truth.

'Gosh, it's so amazing you could come, you know – you really saved my bacon. Usually we take turns to arrange entertainment for the family get-togethers, and I *totally* forgot it was my go this time. But when I ran into you, I was just like: Oh. My. God! Perfect for Halloween, you know? You look fabulous, by the way,' Figgy added, lyingly.

Claire was in the middle of what was turning out to be an indefinitely long lean patch. She was wearing battered trainers with holes in the heels, a pair of black jeans that were so worn through they were grey, and a fifteen-year-old wool coat over her one nice winter jumper, in deference to the fact they were visiting a rich family. Her dyed black hair was showing about three inches of mousy roots, in contrast to Figgy's perfect white-blonde French plait. Figgy wasn't totally unkind. This hadn't stopped Claire asking for a fee about 150 per cent higher than her usual rate, to which Figgy had readily agreed. So readily that Claire realized she should have plumped for 200 per cent.

'Yeah,' she said, offering a smile. 'It should be good. It's a big old house, right?'

'Mmm! It has *wings*. Grade Two listed, because of the library. Of course, really it all belongs to Nana. She keeps joking that she's going to change her will and have Mummy and Daddy out on their ear. They've properly rowed about it a few times, so I hope it doesn't kick off in front of you. That would be so embarrassing! It's just, you know, such an expensive old place to run, and I think Nana is worried that Mummy and Daddy are struggling. But honestly, Mummy would rather sell a kidney than that house.'

There was a pause as Figgy changed up a gear, releasing the clutch so abruptly that Claire jerked forward about six inches and heard one of the bags in the back fall off the seat.

'Whoops! Anyway, you don't need to worry about all that. It's a lovely place, really. I think the house is a couple of hundred years old or something. And the land used to have a monastery, so there are some ruined bits of wall and things that are much older. That's why the house is still officially called The Cloisters.'

'There'd better not be any grim dead monks hanging about,' interjected Sophie from the back.

'There's supposedly *heaps* of ghosts,' said Figgy happily. 'Including this very creepy monk. Every time there's a death, he's meant to appear to the next member of the family who's going to pop their clogs! Although nobody has ever actually seen him – at least not for hundreds of years. Monty made Tristan dress as the monk and hide in my wardrobe once, though, the beast.'

She gave no explanation of who either Tristan or Monty was. Claire imagined some boisterous cousins who visited every summer to have adventures, like the extremely smug children from *The Famous Five*. Boys in knee-shorts and long socks who said 'Rather!' and drank loads of ginger beer and lemonade to wash down doorstep-sized ham sandwiches.

Figgy suddenly swerved right, onto a neat dirt road that sloped downwards. Unidentifiable trees knotted their arms together overhead. The car began scrunching over gravel, and Claire got a glimpse of an imposing grey stone portico, before Figgy swung around the side of the building and came to a stop at the back. There were lights on here – Figgy explained that the family spent most of their time in and around the old kitchen.

'All these bits used to be for, you know, looking after the house,' she said as she got out of the car. 'Pantries, and rooms for some of the important servants, that sort of thing. It's been converted into the family home, so the rest of the place can be used for' – Figgy waved her hands vaguely – 'weddings and corporate away-days and shooting parties, and so on.'

She led them through a heavy green wooden door, which opened directly into a large room with a flagstoned floor and whitewashed walls. Claire was immediately disorientated by the bright light, the explosion of savoury smells and an assault of loud hooting from the family. It was a kind of wordless, elongated vowel noise in place of an actual greeting, to herald their arrival.

A shorter, squatter, older version of Figgy bustled over, though where Figgy's skin was a delicate white porcelain colour with perfect blush cheeks, this woman was more bronzed, as if she spent most weekends gardening. She had a perfect feathery blonde bob and a deep pink cardigan with a string of neat pearls hanging around her neck, but she also had a powerful welly-boots aura. This was not just a mum. This was an M&S mum.

'Hellooooo, dahlings! I'm afraid we couldn't wait to eat, but there's plenty left,' said – presumably – Clementine, giving out air-kisses that left a strong rose-scented perfume in their wake. 'I'll make up some plates. Come in, come in! Say hello. Hugh was just going into the other room to watch the rugger.' Here Clementine gave an exaggerated eyeroll, as if to intimate that they were all girls here – ha, men and their balls!

'That woman never met a Laura Ashley print she didn't like,' said Sophie, talking quietly in Claire's ear. 'I bet she has a knitting circle of dearest friends and hates every one of them. I bet she has a plan to kill each of them and get away with it.'

Sophie had a habit of being unkind about people when she first met them (and also after she'd first met them), but in this case Claire had to admit she was right. Clementine had an intensity to her kindness that hinted at a blanket intensity to all her actions.

They paused to look around. The room they were in was clearly the old kitchen, but had been converted to an all-purpose family room. It had a high ceiling hung with bunches of dried flowers and herbs, and was bright and warm. In front of the door where they'd come in were a couple of creaking armchairs, and a much-loved sofa faced a smouldering fire. A sturdy wooden table ran off to the left, taking up almost the whole length of the rest of the room, towards a large blue Aga at the far end. The table still held the remnants of a family meal, as well as a few remnants of family, who were getting up to be introduced.

In contrast to his wife's crisp consonants, patriarch Hugh's voice was a kind of Canary Wharf foghorn. It went well with his vigorous handshake and his job 'in finance'. He had a ruddy complexion, the pinkish-red inflammation of a white man who drank a lot of red wine and ate a lot of red meat. His watery blue eyes squinted out of a once-handsome face that was losing its definition at the edges, like a soft cheese.

'Hugh looks like a man who never misses an episode of *Question Time*,' murmured Sophie, cocking an eyebrow.

Claire bit on the inside of her cheek, and managed to give a non-committal 'mhmm' in response to Hugh's greeting. He was folding up a broadsheet paper. There was a story with the headline 'I Don't Care What the Wokerati Say, I Won't Stop Putting Mayonnaise in My Welsh Rarebit', and she looked at this in disbelief and confusion for long enough that Hugh noticed.

'Ridiculous, isn't it? Can't do or say anything these days. Corporate political correctness is running amok everywhere, and you can't even bloody eat food how you want!' he said, misreading her expression. 'Now people are complaining that if you make rarebit with mayo, it's cultural appropriation! Can you believe it?'

Claire considered the best way to answer this.

'No,' she said. 'I cannot believe people are doing that.' She was aware that: a) she would probably fall into this newspaper's definition of wokerati; and b) if she was able to conceal this from Hugh like a ratfuck coward, she might be able to get a bonus for good behaviour on top of her already-inflated fee.

'"Putting some mayo in your Welsh rarebit" sounds like a sex thing anyway,' commented Soph. 'Newspaper columnists are all perverts.'

Claire bit the inside of her other cheek. Fortunately, this conversation was rescued by the introduction of a third new family member. Hugh gave an awkward side-arm hug to the newcomer, a woman in her forties. 'This lovely creature is Tuppence. M'boy Monty, my eldest, had the good sense to tie her down!'

Everything about Tuppence was meek: meek ponytail, a swathe of meek pashminas and layered cottons in various browns, and a meek, limp handshake. Even the cold she appeared to have was meek. She kept mopping her nose with tissues that were overflowing from her sleeves, rather than blowing it once, to have done with it.

But when she said, 'It really is nice to meet you!' Claire decided Tuppence was her favourite person in the world. 'My husband can't be here this weekend,' she said, answering a question that Claire had not in fact asked. 'He and Tristan are working on an important case at their firm.'

'Er, sorry – who is Tristan?'

Figgy elbowed in and took Claire's coat. 'Sorry, should have said, darling. Tris is my youngest bro, youngest of the four of us. He's an absolute brat, honestly.'

'They're both lawyers at Monty's firm in London,' said Tuppence. 'But we'll have to make do without them this time, I suppose.'

'Interesting,' whispered Sophie, close to Claire's ear. 'Tuppence actually sounds quite pleased to be rid of Monty. This family is definitely going to turn out to be a mess, I love it. LOL.'

'Most families are a mess,' replied Claire, with an apologetic grimace. 'Uh, I mean... um, organizing events for families, you know – a nightmare.'

To Claire's surprise, Tuppence covered her mouth at this and looked at the ceiling. 'As long as we don't put mayonnaise in the rarebit,' she said, as she looked back at Claire. Claire couldn't have sworn to it, but she thought Tuppence might have winked.

That seemed to be all of the family present in the kitchen. Of Nana, Tuppence's child or the improbable Basher, there was currently no sign. Clementine reappeared, putting down a loaded plate and leading Claire to sit at the table. Sophie stuck her tongue out at the back of Clem's head and declared that she was going to look around – which meant roaming the house to nose through as much of people's private lives as possible.

'So, Claire!' said Hugh, who had conjured a bottle of wine from nowhere. 'Last name Voyant, yes? HA!'

Claire loaded an exploratory forkful of pie, as Figgy sat down next to her. 'Nope. Hendricks. Good one, though.' This was her polite stock response to a joke she had heard about a million, billion times.

Hugh was struggling manfully with the corkscrew, and Clementine took the bottle without speaking and opened it for him. Her expression was dispassionate.

'Terribly exciting, though,' said Clementine, giving a jovial little shrug. 'Very unusual kind of entertainment to do, you know. I was really interested when Figgy said she'd hired you.'

'Mhmm. This pie is really great, thank you,' said Claire, shovelling it down. She was quite hungry because she'd only had a thing of Super Noodles for lunch before she got on the train. In contrast, Figgy was taking small and delicate mouthfuls and savouring each, as if she were a judge on *Masterchef*.

'Claire and I were at university together, d'you remember me saying, Mummy?' said Figgy. 'And I ran into her and, when she told me her job, I thought it would be so quirky and spooky. I was only saying to Claire in the car, it's perfect for Halloween. Didn't I say that, Claire?'

'Yes, you did. And yeah, this is usually quite a good time of year for me.'

Claire noticed that everyone in the room was sort of hanging around, watching her. It was a strange feeling. She didn't think they were trying to be rude, but it seemed a bit like they were privy to a rare zoological exhibit. Just as she thought of them as common-or-garden posh dullards, Claire realized that they saw her as the lesser-known drab weirdo. It wasn't that people didn't think she was weird quite often, but they were usually more subtle about it; or, having hired her, were more engaged with the weirdness. And she had seen enough horror films to know that a bunch of upper-class people inviting you to their family home for Halloween weekend, and then examining you like some sort of game bird, was a potential recipe for disaster. She looked around, but Sophie was still off exploring.

Perhaps realizing that everyone was staring at Claire in silence, Clementine abruptly announced that there wasn't

15

a pudding, but there was fruit, which made Hugh grumble under his breath. He sidled off to watch the rugby. Figgy finished eating and started helping her mother to tidy up, which made Claire feel awkward. She concentrated on her plate instead. Her wine glass kept magically refilling as she ate, and soon she was feeling quite hot and sick from all the carbs and alcohol that she had hoofed into her stomach.

As if sensing this, too, Clementine led her away to a neat twin bedroom. Clementine's powers of observation and/or telepathy were unnerving, but the fact that it was a twin room pleased Claire, because it meant there was enough room for Sophie to keep herself entertained. All the furnishings were cream or white, and the walls and roof were a bit higgledy-piggledy. The walls didn't join up where you'd expect them to – like something a child had tried to make out of Play-Doh. There was a little en suite shower and toilet, though, which was probably more complex than a Play-Doh house would allow. It was very nice. A lot nicer than her flat in London.

Claire opened the window to cool down and suppress her nausea. She was leaning out, collecting deep lungfuls of clean country air, when she realized it wasn't as clean as she'd expected. The dense and delicious smell of weed was wafting through the autumn night. Then she caught the sound of quiet talking and, remarkably, Sophie laughing.

It took her a few minutes of self-consciously creeping around cold corridors in the dark, but eventually Claire found a heavy curtain that was concealing a set of French doors. On the other side of these was a discreet patio, with a couple of tables and chairs and one of those big garden wood-burner things.

Sophie was staring into the flames. Next to her, a teenager with blue hair was clutching an asymmetrical black cardigan around themself and holding about two-thirds of a massive joint.

'All right?' said the teenager, jerking their head up in greeting. They were a good few inches taller than Sophie, looked maybe a couple of years older – enough to legally buy a pint, at least – and appeared to have shaved stripes into one of their eyebrows. 'I'm Alex.'

'Huh, I assumed you were younger. Figgy made it sound as if you're, like, twelve. Are you -andra or -ander?'

'Neither. Does it matter?'

'Nope,' said Claire.

'Cool. Don't tell Granny Clem about the weed.'

Claire thought about this. 'Er. I won't if I can have some.'

'Mutually assured destruction,' said Alex, whilst breathing out another thick herbal cloud. 'I like it.' They passed her the joint and moved away from Sophie to get closer to the fire. Claire took the joint, but exclaimed, 'Fucking Christ!' and nearly dropped it when someone else entirely said, 'You must be Claire.'

Claire leaned over to peer at the other side of the wood-burner. There was a very old lady sitting in a wheelchair, wrapped (as is traditional for little old ladies in wheelchairs) in a couple of tartan blankets. Her eyes were twinkling and she looked very much like she was about to laugh. Leaning on a table near her was a man Claire just

17

about recognized as the Dorito-eater from Figgy's party years ago. He had shaved all his messy blond hair off, which made him look gaunt and tired.

'That's Basher and Nana,' said Sophie. 'They're all right. I like them.'

'I'm right, aren't I?' Nana said. 'You're Claire. Figgy's friend from university.'

'Yeah, that's me,' said Claire. She took a modest hit from the joint and passed it back to Alex. It felt weird smoking weed in front of someone else's granny – great-granny, even. 'Um. Basher and I have actually met before.'

'Hmm,' said Basher. 'I think I remember.'

'Wait, you're the medium?' said Alex, suddenly interested. 'Cool. That's cool. So you can talk to ghosts then.'

'Yup.'

'You really expect us to believe that?' asked Basher.

'Erm, no. Not really. Most people don't, obviously,' said Claire.

Nana laughed and her eyes twinkled again. 'Very good answer. She's got you pegged, Bash, dear.'

'You don't *look* like a medium,' said Alex, passing the joint again.

Emboldened by the positive reception, Claire took a healthier pull this time and spent a few moments looking up at the sky. It had become a very clear night, and this far from a city she could see all the stars scattered everywhere, like broken glass in a pub car park.

'I dunno,' she said after a bit. 'What are mediums supposed to look like?'

'Yeah, all right, fair enough. Do you have a – a what-chamacallit. A spirit guide?'

'Yup, I do.'

Basher snorted at this.

'I do, though!' Claire protested.

'Yes,' Basher said. 'I expect he's some Native American chieftain. Or a poor Victorian shoeshine boy?'

'No, *actually*,' said Claire, who was feeling the effects of what really was very good-quality weed. 'Ah – nah, I don't know if I should tell you.'

'You know you have to now!' cried Alex.

'Yeah, g'wan. It'll freak 'em out,' said Sophie.

'Okay, okay. She's a girl in fact.'

'Ah yes,' said Basher. 'With long dark hair, and she is going to crawl out of the TV?'

'That's a whole other thing. That's a movie – that's not real. Duh,' Claire replied.

'Of course, I apologize. So what is your ghost's tragic back-story? A Georgian waif who died at Christmas? A poor misfortunate who pined to death in the fifties?'

'Don't be boring, Uncle B,' said Alex. 'You sound like Dad when you get all smug.'

'She's not a Victorian waif,' said Claire, who was starting to get a bit annoyed by Basher and was keen to prove him wrong. 'She's from the noughties. She died when she was seventeen.'

'Ah, very convenient,' said Basher. 'No historical research required with a ghost from your own generation.'

'Well, joke's on you, because I studied history, so if I

wanted to make up a period-accurate ghost I could. But I don't need to,' said Claire. She was trying to freak them out a bit, but it wasn't really working.

Sophie rolled her eyes.

Claire looked up at the diamond sky again and started laughing. 'It's funny – she's not anything. She's just normal really.'

'Am *not*, weirdo,' said Sophie. 'I'm exceptional.'

'She's annoying,' Claire corrected. She looked over the flames at her friend, bright-eyed and smirking, standing in the clothes she had been murdered in. 'Her name's Sophie and she's been eavesdropping on you for, like, half an hour already.'

2

A Quick Bit of Seance

The truth was that Claire was not a very good medium. Her figure was not suited to maxi-dresses, incense made her sneeze and she couldn't be arsed with smoky eyeshadow. She also wasn't good at coming up with significant but vague things to say about the afterlife, like 'Ah, the energies from the Other Side are strong here.' The only part she was good at was that she could genuinely see and talk to dead people, but as it turned out, that bit was the least important.

When Claire had turned to freelance mediuming on a full-time basis she'd swiftly discovered that nobody ever wants a real seance. Attempts to do genuine ones usually ended in disappointment and bad reviews on Tripadvisor. Really, punters just wanted something they could tell their friends about.

They did not actually want to talk to their dearly departed grandad who, even if he was still hanging around, would be more likely to ask about Tottenham's form, and complain that they never visited enough when he was alive, than say that he loved them and was happy where he was, in heaven with Jesus and all the angels. In fact the two were mutually exclusive: a ghost could not be both in heaven (or whatever came after dying) and able to have a chat on Earth.

Claire didn't have an especially scientific mind, but as far as she could tell some people simply stayed hanging around after they died, and that was that. It was usually someone who had regrets, either about how they had lived or how they died. Maybe they didn't get to say goodbye to their loved ones, or their cupcake business didn't get as much recognition as they felt it deserved, or one of their family managed to get the standing lamp they'd said they absolutely couldn't have. If they resolved that – if they realized their family loved them anyway, that their cupcakes weren't actually that great, or that the standing lamp was fugly – then they would disappear. If not, they just hung around, making the air cold and sometimes moaning at other ghosts (particularly the case in churchyards, where there were usually a few ghosts corralled together, nurturing petty ghost grievances that were the dead person equivalent of a neighbour not returning a borrowed casserole dish, but sharpened to acuteness over hundreds of years). Unless they made an effort to keep their shit literally together, older ghosts could get fuzzy, and eventually became nothing more than a little cloud of misty unhappiness.

That was how it was; that was what Claire had observed. In the extremely online debates about whether a hot dog was a sandwich, Claire would be the sort of person to say that a sandwich was what got put in front of you when you asked for one in a greasy spoon. Evidence suggested that a ghost was a person capable of annoying nobody except, specifically, Claire, and this rendered the metaphysics of the situation more or less a moot point for her.

Over the years, Sophie and Claire had, using a lot of trial and error, developed what were fairly good versions of fake seances, with a bit of real communication with the dead thrown in – which Claire editorialized and expanded upon, if the ghosts weren't saying anything that interesting or nice. Technically, Claire didn't need Sophie's help to talk to ghosts, but the process (which involved Sophie yelling loudly to attract as many spirits as possible) went more smoothly when they worked together. Claire had an advantage over her spiritualist ancestors: cold-reading was pretty easy when everyone shared everything online, plus Sophie was able to have a good nose around their hosts' houses without anyone knowing.

Their seances were sufficiently skilful now that Claire had a client bench deep enough at least to eat and pay the rent. But she did feel aggrieved that her ability to see and talk to dead people – which was actually a pretty bloody impressive thing to do, when you thought about it – was basically good for nothing. By rights she should be mega-rich and have a syndicated television show. But she wasn't and she didn't, and even if someone offered her a TV gig, she would get scared and turn it down, partly for reasons she didn't like to talk about which had left her afraid of public exposure, but also because she didn't have the natural confidence around people that Sophie did. Sometimes, in very quiet moments at two o'clock in the morning, Claire wondered if it would have been better if *she* had died and become the ghost. Sophie would probably have had a recurring guest spot on *This Morning* by now. All Claire had was this gig at Figgy's parents' weird old house.

And she was possibly jeopardizing even that by chuckling like a gibbon after describing how a girl had died at seventeen and was now her invisible companion.

'Sorry, sorry,' she said, getting herself under control. 'It's just funny that you're saying she doesn't exist, when she's right there.'

Alex, Basher and Nana looked, variously, alarmed, incredulous and sympathetic.

'Seventeen! That's no age,' said Nana. 'I'm sorry to hear that, Sophie dear.' She looked towards where she assumed Sophie was standing, and Sophie obligingly moved so that she wasn't wrong. 'Did you two know each other when you were alive?'

'No-o-o. No. Nope,' said Claire. She had learned from experience that people didn't respond well to her spirit guide being her best friend from school, a real person whose memory Claire was – to the outside observer – exploiting for money. 'We would have been born around the same time, but that's it. Never knew her. She just, uh, turned up one day. It was when I was a teenager, too, so we suspect it was something to do with hormones and, er, moon energies.'

Sophie grimaced. 'You know, I still hate it that that line actually works on people.'

'A bit like the X-Men,' said Alex, snickering. 'In the films a lot of them got powers around the age of sexual maturity. Is seeing ghosts also a metaphor, do you think?'

'I think I understand that. I got a lot of stretchmarks when I turned sixteen. I grew about a foot overnight, I remember,' said Nana.

'Oh, come on, Nana. You don't seriously believe any of this is true?' said Basher, who seemed to be getting annoyed. He would be the useful sceptic, Claire could already tell. 'Not the stretchmarks. The talking to ghosts.'

'Well, I'm very nearly dead, dear, and you're talking to me,' Nana said.

'Before you arrived,' Sophie told Claire, 'they were talking about how the family should just sell the house to a hotel chain that's sniffing around. Du-something. Du Lotte Hotels, I think.' Claire repeated this.

'That doesn't prove anything!' said Basher, his eyes flashing in the firelight. 'You probably heard that yourself. And by the way, it's bloody rude to listen in to private conversations.'

Sophie moved around to blow on his neck idly and make him shiver, and giggled when he did.

'That's her. She's blowing on your neck.'

'Give over. It's cold out here – I am cold.'

Sophie next started tickling the side of Nana's face. Nana raised a hand to her cheek.

'Yeah, that's her,' said Claire, before Nana could ask. 'She's tickling your face.' Claire elaborated, explaining: Sophie wasn't a poltergeist, she couldn't pick things up or rifle through your knicker drawer, but if you'd left your knicker drawer open or a private letter out somewhere, she'd have a proper good look. She'd been naturally nosy even before she'd died; being invisible only made it easier. If she blew on your face, it felt like you were looking into a freezer; and if she tickled your cheek, you might think a cold spider was walking across it. But that was all she could do, unless she was getting help from Claire.

'That's jolly interesting, isn't it?' said Nana. 'Do you know, I'm quite looking forward to dying now. I'm sure ghosts don't get swollen feet.'

'First of all,' said Basher, 'can we stop talking as if you're going to shuffle off your mortal coil tomorrow morning? And, second, have we just accepted the existence of ghosts now? Is that all it took?'

Alex shrugged and carefully put out the joint. 'We should do a seance. Can we do a seance? I've never done one before, I wanna do one.'

'Doing one tomorrow night. S'what I'm here for. What *we're* here for. When all the other guests have arrived. Midnight seance: bell, book and candle, the whole thing. Well spooky. Proper seance business.'

'I mean we should do one *tonight*. Now.'

Claire looked over at Sophie.

26

'*I* don't care if we do one now,' Sophie said. 'Figgy was right: there are a load of deados hanging around, for me to drum up for conversation. An old lady was having a blazing row with a little Frenchman in one of the rooms in the big house. Also a pervy old gardener, like, you know, a really shit version of Sean Bean in that TV series about a woman shagging her gamekeeper. On the other hand, they seem quite boring, they might not turn up, and you're pissed and also high, so I dunno if you'll be much use at cold-reading, if the ghosts are rubbish. It's a gamble. But one I'm willing for you to take. LOL.'

Alex misinterpreted the long pause while Claire listened to Soph, because they tipped their head on one side and said, 'I'll pay you extra, if that's what you're worried about. Half fee on top again, right? Exclusive preview for the family, which all our horrible godparents and Grandad Hugh's mates from work don't get when they turn up tomorrow.'

Claire had *not* been worried about getting paid extra, and then worried that she hadn't worried about it, because that meant she really was quite high.

'That means,' added Basher with a slight smile, 'Alex is going to persuade someone else to pay you extra.'

'Potato, pot*ah*to's rich lawyer dad,' said Alex, flapping their hand impatiently.

Claire opened her mouth to object, then shut it again, and Alex took advantage of this indecision. They bundled her back inside and into the kitchen, and before long had convinced Clementine and Figgy that they could have

27

what Clementine called 'a quick bit of seance' before bed, as long as Nana didn't get too worked up. They went to crowbar Hugh from his game ('For heaven's sake, it's a recording, Hugh! You can just pause it!') and Claire went to her room to try and prepare as best she could.

She filled the sink with cold water and stuck her face into it, while Sophie lay on one of the beds and watched.

'You're such a train wreck. You haven't done one of these while you're pissed since like, what... 2013? This is going to go terribly – it's going to be amazing.'

'"Bit of seance",' Claire muttered. 'It's not a sugar-free fizzy drink. You can't do a... a fucking "seance lite". Christ, I hate rich people.'

'You know, I'm not even sure they're that rich, really,' said Soph, thinking out loud. 'I mean obviously they *are*, in a relative sense, but if you look around at this place, you start to notice all the bits where it's falling apart.' She pointed out cracks in the plaster around the window, and patches of rot in the wooden frame itself.

Sophie was much better at noticing things. All she did now was watch, of course, but she had watched when she was alive, too. She had noticed, for example, the introverted, mousy girl nervously waiting alone at the bus stop on the first day of Big School at the turn of the millennium, and although Soph had been alone as well, she had not been nervous. It was an emotion that was beyond her, even aged eleven. She had gone up to Claire and said, 'Hello. Let's be friends.' And so they were. Claire had never been sure why she'd been chosen, but it had happened. And Sophie was pretty, and knew how to plait her hair and do make-up, and already shaved her legs, and pretended not to try in class, even though she secretly did. Her association threw a shield around Claire, who suspected she would otherwise have been consigned to the weirdo kids who wore bow ties and wrote poetry at lunchtime.

In return, Claire helped Sophie with homework – which was the sort of thing Sophie never had the patience for – and made her laugh, and bared her secret innermost thoughts and listened to Sophie's, and drank blue WKD in a field until they were sick, and swung on children's swings on frosty nights until they went so high that Claire was afraid of what would happen if they fell.

Soph was never afraid. She would always have kept going.

As they got older, Sophie decided her favourite drink was Bacardi, and that was what she was like, too: strong, sweet, clear, overwhelming. (Claire was rosé wine, something a bit childish masquerading as almost adult.)

When Sophie vanished, Claire had lost touch with who she was as a person. The disappearance had given her, by association, a layer of grim, Gothic mystique. The missing girl's best friend! The *enfant tragique*! But after a while everyone had tired of that and had dropped Claire, for her rapidly increasing strangeness: the talking to herself, the covering her ears to block out inaudible sounds, the wearing of layers and layers of clothes even indoors, and then the eventual embracing of the cold. Because Sophie had come back. Like she had chosen Claire all over again. Sophie was the first friend Claire had, and the first ghost she saw. After she returned, Claire saw dead people everywhere.

Secretly she had been relieved at Sophie's return – even in her ghostly state. But lately, although she'd never share the thought, Claire had begun to wonder how much she and Sophie really had in common, apart from the fact that they'd been friends for so long. Perhaps, under normal circumstances, their friendship would not have survived the test of adulthood. Luckily – or, technically unluckily, she supposed – any testing was now moot. They were stuck together. Almost literally, because unlike most ghosts who were tethered to a place, Sophie was tethered to Claire, and when they got far enough apart Claire could feel it like tension on a lead.

Worse, perhaps, was that Sophie was stuck as a person, too: she had the lifetime of experience of an adult, but assessed it like a teen. She was quick to anger, quick to invent and point out injustices, as swift and as casual in her insults as she had been when part of a tribe of adolescents, picking sides and drawing battle lines at house-parties and pubs. More and more, Claire worried that she herself was the same. Perhaps she had never got rid of her worst, most immature impulses because they were given voice and form every day. They were there when she woke up and when she got into bed, and they watched her while she dreamed.

*

Left alone in her guest bedroom, Claire changed into what she thought of as her work clothes: a sober black dress and, retrieved reverentially from a plastic baggy that years ago had held a small quantity of terrible cheap cocaine that was later snorted off a toilet in a student union bar, one of Sophie's real-life butterfly hair-claws. Claire carefully fixed it into her own hair, pinning back the wonky bit of her fringe left from where she'd tried to trim it herself. Then she gathered her equipment: a big brass hand-bell, a heavy silver candlestick with impressive wax dribbles, a plastic Bic lighter and a large, old Bible.

The main house would normally have been hosting guests or some kind of event, but was kept free on birthday weekends so that the Wellington-Forges could pretend it was still all theirs. That they had the run of the whole place and bossed servants about, like their ancestors used to. The bit of seance was going to be held in the library, an impressive room with floor-to-ceiling shelves on one wall, full of leather-bound books with gold-printed spines: bottle-green, wine-red, earthy brown tomes. Opposite these was a bank of huge leaded-glass windows.

The clouds peeled back from the moon outside, and the room was filled with little diamonds of black and white. Claire felt her skin tingle, like she was being watched. She breathed in and, instead of the dry air of a room full of books, she tasted mud in the back of her throat. Her heart rate spiked in sudden panic and she was struck with a wave of fear and nausea – a nausea distinct from the churning red wine sickness she already felt. Sharp pain flashed behind her eyes and she groped for the back of a chair to lean on.

There was a sudden rattle as Figgy started to pull the curtains shut, and Clementine switched a lamp on. The moment was over, and nobody seemed to have noticed. Claire looked at Sophie, who nodded grimly.

'I felt it too,' she said. 'I'll keep an eye out for any buzz kills.' Some spirits stayed bitter. The mean ones did try to ruin things sometimes.

The family were arranged around a large round table. Nana patted a seat between her and Basher. Claire went over, placed the candle and book in front of her, then bent to put the bell under the table in a slow, exaggerated fashion.

'Hold on,' said Basher, on cue. 'I read about this. Houdini showed how you can just ring the bell with your foot and we wouldn't know.'

Claire tried not to smile. She could always count on one person knowing about Houdini. 'Of course,' she said and put the bell in the middle of the table. She nodded to herself, turned the lamp off and then regretted the order in which she'd done things, as she blundered back to the table in darkness to light the candle.

The room narrowed to a point as the darkness became darker. As if they knew what was expected of them, everyone took the hands of the people on either side of them.

Sophie knelt in the centre of the table, her pale face illuminated from below by the flame. She crawled forward until she was on top of it, and the candle burned inside her. Everyone else saw the candle begin to burn blue at the

32

edges and throw strange, refracted shadows that danced on the ceiling and walls where they had no business being. Claire saw her friend glowing like a paper lantern. She saw the pink hair-claw that she now wore mirrored in Sophie's hair, the ghost of a hair-clip. It was here, but also there. It was in two places at once. This always made her feel weird.

Claire leaned forward and bowed her head, and Sophie reached out and put her hand on top of it. It was like someone had plonked a bag of frozen peas on the crown of Claire's head, and she couldn't help shivering. She felt the *zip* of the connection between them, like she was a battery pack and Sophie was an iPhone that had just been plugged in. She fought the urge to yawn.

'Line!' said Soph.

'Mmm? Wzt?'

'It's your line, weirdo. "Sophie, spirit guide, lost souls of this place, yadda-yadda, and so on." You are useless.'

Claire stifled a burp. 'S-Sophie. My spirit guide. Please – ugh – please connect us to the lost souls of this place. Help us speak with them. Is there anybody there?'

Sophie reached in front of her and, by using Claire's strength, was able to lift the bell about half an inch. She began ringing it gently, but rhythmically. Claire was pleased to hear several gasps from around the table. They would have been less impressed by the mystic forces at work if they could hear Sophie's yelling: 'COME ON THEN! BRING OUT YER DEAD! LET'S GO! TALKING TO THE LIVING, RIGHT HERE! ROLL UP, ROLL UP – I'VE NOT GOT ALL FUCKING NIGHT.'

A few foggy shapes began to seep through the walls – the really old dead, who couldn't remember who or what they were any more. Only one ghost who turned up still looked like a person: an elderly white man with a green flat cap, a big white moustache and yellow corduroy trousers. He was leaning on a pitchfork.

'Here,' he said, in a strong Cornish accent. 'Can us really talk to them? Ask about the girl who visited last year. Where's she to? She had a cracking pair of—'

'Ohmigod, shutthefuckup, you old perv! I think he's your lot tonight, to be honest,' Sophie told Claire, apologetically. 'Go with an old standby. I haven't discovered anything properly juicy yet.'

They fumbled through a few cold-reads, based on family photos that Sophie described, and the people round the table were more or less impressed by the whole thing (mostly less, if Claire was being honest with herself). Sophie kept laughing and suggesting she reveal that Tuppence was going to cheat on Monty and abscond to the Lake District with her lover and all the family's money. Getting desperate, Claire tried intimating that Clementine's father gave the family their blessing to sell the house, which went down extremely poorly. Basher's hand tightened angrily in her own. But at that point the old gardener, who was still hanging around, got bored. He hobbled forward and grabbed Sophie's ankle with an experimental air. Claire felt another *zip* as the drain on her doubled, and then a ghostly argument rang out across the silent room, for everyone to hear.

'How does this work? Tell them we don't like all the young lads who comes here and has big parties and pisses in the rose garden. Ruins the soil.'

'*Ohmigod*, let go, that is *so* rude!'

Claire craned to try and see what was happening, because no ghost had done this to Sophie before. None of the family around the table had leapt from their seat in alarm, so she was fairly sure the ghosts weren't visible to anyone else, but the old man was definitely pulling energy from her through Sophie, because she could feel herself getting more tired by the second.

Claire could just about see that Hugh and Clementine, off to her left, were looking around to try to locate the source of the voices. Normally dead people sounded sort of two-dimensional – not without emotion, but flat, appearing in Claire's ears without bumping into any air in between. It was hard to tell, but now it was as if someone had turned on an invisible speaker above the table, so that Sophie's and the gardener's voices were being pumped into the room, echoing off the walls, crossing over one another and wavering in volume.

'Also, please tell Her Majesty congratulations on the birth of her son. I would have written, but I couldn't, on account of being dead.'

'Okay, well, you could mean literally, like, three differ-ent people by that, so I don't know—'

'You button up, young lady. Trouble is that young people like you got no respect for their elders, so you just let me talk—'

'Claire, this grotey old perv won't let go of my *foot*.'

Nana started laughing.

'Well! Is that Miss Janey?' asked the gardener, ignoring Sophie's attempts to kick him off her. 'You know, I always took an interest in you – a very particular interest. Bright as a button you were.'

'Hello, Ted! I'm glad you still seem to be in good form. For a dead man,' said Nana.

'Ar, good form, Miss Janey, good form.' Ted was starting to look alarmingly *solid*.

Claire felt light-headed. Basher was leaning forward.

'And may I say you looked beautiful on your wedding day. You were a fine girl and, if I may add, meaning no disrespect, you grew up into *a very fine young woman*—'

Sophie shrieking 'Ohmi*god*, put a fucking cork in it, Ted!' was the last thing the party heard, before Claire jerked her head back from Sophie's reach. It was like unplugging a really strange and specific radio. But *she* could still see and hear the ghosts. Sophie was kicking at Ted while he cackled heartily.

'The, uh, the circle is broken, or whatever,' said Claire vaguely. She blew out the candle. The darkness was reassuringly normal and gave her a few moments of cover to slump back in the chair. She would say it felt as if she'd just run a marathon – if she had ever done any recreational running whatsoever.

Around her she could hear the Wellington-Forges reacting. Figgy was doing happy piglet squeals, enjoying being scared in a safe way. Hugh kept rumbling, 'Very good. Bloody good, I thought.' Nana was humming. Clementine immediately began bustling, and soon had the lights on again. This revealed that Alex was on their hands and knees under the table, and Basher was pulling large books off a shelf at random.

Alex poked their head out and looked up at Claire, unabashed. 'No wires,' they said, with a grin.

'That does not rule out wireless technology,' said Basher. He continued feeling along the shelves and checking books.

'Ah,' said Claire. 'You're, er, looking for a speaker.' At least she tried to say this, but the word 'speaker' disappeared into a yawn.

'You should go to bed,' said Sophie. 'This idiot properly wiped you out. Could have hurt you. D'you hear me? Look at her.' She glared at Ted, who took his cap off and wrung it in his hands in such a cartoonishly subservient way that it looped round into sarcasm. He walked out into the garden through the wall.

'Well now, that was fun!' said Clementine. 'But you look tired, darling. Don't let us keep you up before the big day tomorrow! And you too, Mum,' she added, turning to Nana.

'Yes, I do think it's time for me to turn in,' agreed Nana. 'I'll be up past my bedtime tomorrow, too!'

They all started to troop out of the room. Claire thought she was last out and pulled the door almost to behind her, but then Soph gave her a nudge. 'Here, look,' she said and pointed back into the library. Claire peered around the door.

Basher had lingered and was standing by the table. He looked around and, satisfied that nobody was watching, waved a hand cautiously through the air where Ted the gardener had been standing during the seance. Then he sighed and seemed to sort of pull himself together. Claire hurried away before he spotted her.

Nana insisted that Claire escort her to bed, although Basher caught up and followed them suspiciously.

'Ted was the gardener here when I was little,' Nana said. 'He died in the middle of turning over potatoes. How extraordinary!'

Claire helped her into bed, while Sophie sat on the end of it, looking at her. Nana had hair like very fine silvery cobwebs, and her skin had shrunk close to her bones, which felt light and breakable like fine china. Claire looked at the veins on the backs of her hands and saw that Nana had very bad arthritis, too. She must be in quite a lot of pain all the time, but didn't show any sign of it. And her eyes, stormy and grey, flashed quick with intelligence. Nothing got past Nana.

'I'm so pleased we'll be doing another one of those tomorrow, dear. That was fantastic! Don't you think so, Basher?'

'Hmm. Yes, fantastic. Unbelievable, one might say,' said Basher, hardly dripping with sincerity. 'But you should get some sleep now, Nana. You have your party tomorrow.'

'Yes, yes. Because, apparently, I *won't* sleep when I'm dead! Ha-ha!'

38

'I don't think Nana will become a ghost,' said Sophie. 'She's too content. She seems quite ready to go. Whenever it happens.'

Claire relayed this, and Nana agreed.

'I do wish, though,' she said, 'that I had sold this place when I had the chance. I kept trying to arrange it, and Clemmy kept putting me off. "The estate agent people couldn't come today" – that sort of thing. It's a millstone in this day and age, you know, a big place like this. Well, I still have time to get it done. I'm going to really push for it. It's still my house, after all.'

Basher carefully tucked his nana in and she snuggled down into the pillows. As she was leaving, Nana grabbed Claire's hand. 'You're a nice girl, Claire. Let's talk more tomorrow.'

Basher helped Claire find her way back to her room, which she was happy about because the corridors all looked the same to her. At one point she tried to open the wrong door, and Basher steered her away, one hand on her elbow. His fingers were long and fine, and his grip was firm but careful – gentle.

'Um. Thank you,' she said.

'Don't mention it. This is not the most normal of houses. But great for Hide and Seek.'

'Were you good at it?'

'Very,' he said, with a smile. Claire imagined he was. Basher was thoughtful and sceptical and thorough. The sort of kid who'd search one room at a time, pulling all the cushions off the sofa before moving on to the kitchen.

He stopped and opened a door to reveal Claire and Sophie's room.

'Thank you again,' said Claire. 'Er. Goodnight. See you tomorrow.'

But Basher lingered in the doorway. 'Listen,' he said, suddenly very serious. 'I cannot explain how you did that right now, but it doesn't mean that I *will* not. And I want you to know that I don't really care if you play cruel tricks on the rest of my family, but do not do it to her.'

'Who?' asked Claire, all innocence.

'You have no poker face, weirdo,' said Sophie, who was leaning against the wall to watch. 'You know exactly who he's talking about.'

'Nana. It's her birthday.'

'I know it's her birthday – that's the whole reason I'm here.'

'You know what I mean. Don't tell Nana she's talking to her parents or her sister, or anything like that.'

'I wouldn't do that. I'm not actually a horrible person,' Claire protested.

'You told her you were passing on a message from her dead husband, though.'

'Er. I mean, yes, I did, but it wasn't a—'

'And it sounded a lot like you were riffing on something Figgy might have told you.'

'Rumbled,' said Sophie, who had a faint smile on her face.

'Well, I… Look, um.' Basher raised an eyebrow and Claire floundered. He was right was the frustrating thing, but she *could* talk to dead people, and it wasn't as if her bit of ad-libbing was really that bad, because Nana wanted to sell the house. Claire felt like she was getting a telling-off from a smug uncle, which seemed very unfair when Basher was in fact a couple of years younger than she was.

'It is her birthday,' he said again, embarrassingly earnest. 'She is old. Leave Nana alone.'

Claire held up both her hands. 'All right, all right – you got me. Don't arrest me. Oh, wait, you can't.' She was snapping back at him like a sulky child, and regretted it straight away.

Basher looked genuinely hurt. He stared at Claire, chewing on the inside of his lip for a few seconds. 'Fuck you,' he said. 'Absolutely fuck yourself.'

He almost slammed the door, but at the last second stopped short. It shut in Claire's face with a sharp click.

In the end, Basher needn't have worried. There was no chance Nana would become upset by Claire's messages from the Other Side. She wouldn't fret any more about selling the house. She wouldn't even get another chat with Ted.

The next morning, Nana was dead.

3

The Body in the Library

Claire was sitting on a wooden bench facing the garden, wearing all her warmest clothes at once. It was mid-morning, but the day was sufficiently grey and grim that the sun hadn't managed to wake up properly. There was still a mist low on the fields in the distance, and everything was damp. She was smoking a cigarette – one of her last – without enthusiasm, and generally trying to stay out of the way. At some point she had acquired a slice of toast. She munched on it rhythmically, between drags on the cigarette, like a cow chewing cud. Ted the ex-gardener was sitting next to her. He seemed to have developed an attachment to her and Sophie.

'I don't know,' he said, jutting his lip out. 'Don't seem right. Don't seem like her time.'

'That's not a thing, Ted. People die when they die.'

But although she was trying to avoid thinking about it, Claire had to admit it felt a bit neat. Old, infirm ladies die in their sleep all the time – it's an occupational hazard of being elderly, exacerbated by how many naps old people take. And yet...

Nana had apparently been found by her daughter, peaceful and cold in bed, when Clementine went to wake her up with a cup of tea. After that, everything became a weird flurry of inaction: people either being busily upset or sitting around not knowing what to do. Claire had sat with Figgy for a bit, making a cursory attempt to comfort her, but it had mostly been excruciatingly long silences until Figgy asked to be left alone. Once rebuffed, Claire extricated herself quietly. She was clearly not supposed to be here, but felt too awkward to approach someone to ask how to leave. Or how she was going to get paid, which was worse. And she still had no phone signal. Couldn't even download her podcasts.

Soph had been roaming around the place most of the morning. There had been little tugs on the connection between them every so often, but now Claire felt it slacken. Sure enough, Sophie walked out of the back door and came over to her.

'Can't find her in there,' she said. 'I'm pretty sure she's gone.'

'G'morning, Miss—'

'Fuck off, Ted.'

'Ted thinks Nana might have been done in before her time,' said Claire gloomily. 'I bet loads of rich people have smothered their grannies. Who would check?'

Ted nodded sagely.

Claire decided to get some blood back into her chilled limbs, so they walked around the outside of the house. The old servants' area, where the family now lived, was a sort of annexe on one side, like a cluster of different-sized barnacles on the bum of a majestic cruise liner. If you looked at the house from the back, it was on the left side, and was partially obscured by a tall box hedge. This was mirrored on the right-hand side, where another hedge stood in front of what Ted said was the rose garden – his pride and joy, when he was alive. He kept up an unceasing monologue of complaints about every gardener who had dared to step foot on the property since him.

The layout meant that, when standing in the gardens and looking back, the big, imposing grey block of a house was symmetrical, with a grand doorway flanked by identical rows of windows on either side. Sophie pointed out the library windows (bottom right), the old dining room that doubled as a kind of ballroom (bottom left), and described the rest of the house as 'just loads of fucking, different-coloured sitting rooms and four-poster beds'. From the back door, a wide patio and shallow stone steps led down to some depressed-looking empty flower beds and more box hedges, these ones about knee-high. There was a big lawn beyond that, stretching off to some trees in the distance.

Claire lit a fresh cigarette and strode down the steps and towards the treeline. 'The thing is,' she said. 'The thing *is*... that it does make sense, doesn't it? Old lady – legal owner of an estate that will pass to her family

– dies immediately after she tells a stranger that she's going to sell to the luxury hotel chain sniffing around, thus doing the family out of—'

'Out of a massive, mouldy old drain on the bank balance?' interrupted Sophie. 'For God's sake, Claire.'

'Yeah, but it's not necessarily about that, is it? It's about, you know, honour and... and tradition. Posh people are all mental about that stuff,' Claire replied.

Ted agreed enthusiastically.

Claire had always secretly thought she'd be quite good at solving crimes. She listened to three different true-crime podcasts, and her favourite TV show was *Murder Profile*, an American police procedural about a murderer-catchin' team made up of people who were all FBI agents and expert psychologists, as well as unbelievably attractive. Sophie found it incredibly boring because every episode had a very similar pattern; you could tell who the murderer was based on who appeared on screen when. But that was why Claire liked it. It was comforting to think that people were predictable even when they were creepy killers. It was, she argued, just like their seances. Patterns of behaviour. And death.

Claire warmed to her subject and started waving her arms around, describing and inventing ways in which everyone in the house could conceivably be a suspect, after the seance: Clementine would apparently sell her organs before she was forced to sell the house, so offing her mum wasn't much of a step; Hugh was probably having an affair with his secretary and, if Nana had found out, he would have needed to kill her before she revealed all; Figgy might be in for a chunk of inheritance in Nana's will, and there was no way that general fannying around in Carnaby Street generated enough income to pay for fashion-onesies and expensive hair salons. Plus Basher had witnessed the conversation at bedtime when Nana had talked about making another push to sell the house, so he could be in it with Clementine. 'Or *he* could have done it alone! You never know. Basher seems quite normal, but scratch the surface of an old family and inbreeding starts pouring out! Plus, as a former copper, he'd know exactly how to—'

But at that moment the ground vanished from beneath Claire's feet. As she fell she let out a kind of strangled squawk, like a surprised chicken. She found herself lying flat on her face and rolled over to look up at the two ghosts, who appeared to be standing on top of a wall that hadn't been there a second ago.

'Ha-ha,' said Ted placidly.

'Piss off,' she said, as soon as she got her breath back. He gave her a look that was old-fashioned, even on a man who'd been dead for decades.

'No,' he said, very patiently, as if talking to a child. '*This* is a ha-ha. Stops sheep and that coming into the garden, but don't spoil the view with a bloody great wall. S'called a ha-ha cos you're surprised when you fall in it.'

'Then it should be called a "bleeding hell" or an "ah shit!", shouldn't it?' Claire stood up and mourned the loss of her precious cigarette. Ted and Sophie weren't on a wall.

They stood on solid ground, but Claire had fallen into a sort of trench about six feet deep (or tall, depending on your point of view) that ran the width of the lawn as far as she could see on either side. The vertical face of the trench was a rough brick wall, and from the bottom of this the ground sloped upwards again, until the lawn continued at almost the same height as before. It was nearly impossible to see the ha-ha until you were right on top of it. Or in it.

Ted pointed further down the trench. There were some bricks set sideways in the wall to use as a kind of ladder. Claire stumped along towards them and eyed the occasional slippery grey rock that poked mutinously out of the nettles at the bottom of the ditch. She could have landed on one of those. Trust the rich to build an architectural death-trap into their lawns, just so they wouldn't have to look at poor people or animals. In fact lawns themselves were simply a grim colonial hangover. *Ooh, look at me, I'm so rich I don't even need to put all this space that I own to any practical use – now how many Irish peasants did we starve today?*

A couple of sheep were looking at Claire with ovine disinterest, as if idiot townies fell into their field all the time. One of them went: *MURRRRRRRM.*

Claire stuck her tongue out at it. The sheep were probably only there for show anyway. Behind them, mist was still clearing from between the trunks of bare trees, the drifts of dead leaves and scrubby brambles.

There was also, it took Claire a moment to realize, a figure standing right in front of the copse. At this distance it was hard to make out amid the trees, especially because it was so straight and still, and the same indistinct, wintery colour as the bark. But once she saw it, she could not unsee it: a hooded, imposing person, staring at her from the black void of their cowl.

As she watched, they raised a long, imperious arm and pointed straight at her. Then, with the same unstoppable yet excruciating slowness of the *Titanic* scraping the side of the iceberg, they pointed off to the side, further back into the hidden depths of the grounds. Claire felt her brain fighting the urge to put a horror movie dolly zoom over the scene, like on the beach in *Jaws*. She shivered.

It was a ghost, of course. Sophie was resolutely unspooked and yawned with great theatricality.

'I suppose it's a choice, isn't it? But it's not very original,' she said.

'That's Brother Simeon,' said Ted, equally unmoved. 'Gloomy old bugger. He's probably the oldest of us still hanging around. He's a family legend, on account of having frightened some people to death a few hundred years back. Used to try and comfort people after funerals, right? Being a monk and all. But some bloody great dead monk turns up after your son dies – that'll give some people a bad turn.'

'Ohhh, yeah. Figgy mentioned it,' said Claire. She was impressed, though. You didn't meet many ghosts who could actually incorporate and appear to the living. She and Sophie still hadn't exactly figured out how that worked, either, but it did happen, and it definitely took a lot of effort. Claire's theory was that the living person needed to sort of *expect* to see them, too, which was why, since fewer people actively believed that ghosts were real in the twenty-first century, people saw them less and less. A monk wandering around a place reputed to be haunted by a monk would just about do it, though.

Brother Simeon still had his arm raised.

'What's he pointing at?' Claire asked Ted.

'The old ruins. S'where The Cloisters gets its name from. He wanders about them most of the time, not talking to any of us. Stuck up, if you ask me.'

Claire surveyed Brother Simeon critically, then cupped her hands around her mouth. 'Oi! What. Do. You. Want?' she called.

But Simeon merely started to glide, with much ominous presentiment, back to his haunt. The effect was only slightly spoiled when he floated through the sheep.

Claire shrugged – suit yourself, mate – and turned to haul herself back onto the top lawn. As she threw her arms onto the grass, she caught sight of someone else walking towards the rose garden. She could barely make them out, and she realized it was another ghost. The place was lousy with them, it seemed.

In contrast to the living, ghosts were harder to see in daylight. She squinted. 'If the silent sheep-botherer was the local mad monk, then who's *that*?' she asked.

Sophie turned to look, too, and after a couple of seconds she exclaimed, 'No way!' and started marching quickly back to the house.

'Sophie! SOPH! Wait for me!'

Claire had to jog to catch up, and by the time they made it around the side of the house to the rose garden, she was out of breath and had a stitch in her side. It was all right for the dead.

The rose garden was, like much of the estate, a bit of a sorry sight in autumn. It was a walled garden designed to be a suntrap, but roses aren't evergreen and the plants had been pruned back for winter, so it was basically a garden of dead sticks. There was a mildewy wooden pergola that probably trailed flowers at other times of the year, with a heavy stone bench under it.

'What? What's the matter?' Claire gasped, bending over and knackered out. When she looked up she gasped again and started off a coughing fit in her shock. Nana was sitting on the bench. She smiled and patted the space next to her.

'I knew it! I knew you'd have unfinished business! Ted said – wait, where's Ted gone? Anyway Ted said, he reckoned – *thought* that—'

Nana raised a faintly see-through hand, calmingly. She looked healthier. Her face was fuller, and she had clearly been right about her sore feet. 'I'm sure you think you know what happened, dear, but you're not right about everything. I wasn't suffocated. Nobody put poison in the glass of water by my bed. I just died, like most old people do.'

'But you were going to sell the house! Hugh is probably having an affair!'

Nana looked a bit confused by this. 'I don't know about that. Although I suppose if Hugh were having an affair, I wouldn't be wholly surprised. But I do have what I think you would call some unfinished business.'

'Ooh, fun!' said Sophie. 'What is it?'

'Well, I'm afraid you're right, in a way. I think that my family did kill someone – but someone else.'

Claire tried to formulate a response to this, but her brain seemed to have short-circuited. Theorizing that Nana had been murdered had been, you know, sort of fun. A game. It wasn't real. But this wasn't fun. This was weird. It went against the usual social norms, even for dead people.

She scratched the back of her head, looked up at the sky and then at the ground, trying to find a way to reboot.

'I... sorry... Sorry, what the *fuck*?'

Nana sighed. 'You know, I thought we had done all right with them. It's very disappointing.'

'What do you mean, Nana?' asked Sophie, who had caught up much more quickly.

'Look into the library, dear.'

Nana pointed to a nearby window in the imposing grey wall of the house, so Claire ambled over. This was the short end of the library, furnished with an end-table and a couple of armchairs. It was hard to see anything beyond that; nobody had opened the curtains at the front of the house since the night before, and the room was so long that the far end of it was in almost total darkness. But she could see something moving around, stumbling a bit as they came closer. They seemed to be clutching their head in their hands and wheeled here and there, criss-crossing the floor with no real purpose, like a wounded animal trying to outrun the pain.

Claire's scalp began to tingle. Just like the night before, she felt nausea rise in her like a wave. Her pulse leapt and she tasted dirt and mould. She wanted, more than anything, to look away, but she couldn't.

It was a ghost, and they were thin. Very thin. Too thin. As the figure loomed towards the light of the window she finally saw: they were bones.

It was a skeleton. But they were still... juicy. Claire could make out patches of flesh melded to the arms and legs, and sagging across the jutting ribs. The crown of their skull glistened and the tips of their fingers clicked as they clawed at it. Straggling fibres of long hair came away as they did so, dropping like wet string.

Claire gagged. She started to shake uncontrollably, panicking but rooted to the spot, deathly afraid, but also unbearably sad. Pain crackled through her head and then returned to stay, sharp and increasing, like someone was worming a needle around behind her eyes. Her legs began to shake. She was about ten seconds away from a dead faint.

The skeleton in the library paused in their terrible, questing walk. They turned, their jaw gaping over-wide in a wordless, tongueless scream, and suddenly Claire was looking straight into the empty void of their eye sockets. They swallowed her whole.

When Sophie had disappeared all those years ago, Claire had of course been sad, but when you're young and healthy, death is something that happens to other people. And now Claire was not a stranger to death. She lived in its chill, looked into its many faces every day. She walked by taxi drivers on Oxford Street who were now far beyond the effects of the massive heart attack that had killed them in their sleep; by victims of violent crime who bore, philosophically, the bloody wounds that lingered into forever. She saw the sad, grey ghosts on the Thames, who waded in and out of the water at Battersea, never far beyond the reach of the river. Ever since Sophie had come back, Claire had been able to see them all, and she wasn't afraid because it was normal now. It was a mundane tragedy. A stubbed toe, a bitten tongue. The sleeping bag in the shop doorway that you walk past every day.

The death staring at her from the library was horror. Agony. Trapped, alone, in your own pain. For all time, where time meant nothing. Claire felt herself disappearing into that misery, and experienced terror. Undiluted fear.

She was afraid, so afraid. For the first time in her entire life, she was completely and totally afraid to die. The effort to turn away was almost beyond her.

Somehow, eyes watering, heart pounding, she managed to jerk herself backwards and away from the window. She fell, shaking, retching into the dead flower beds. Sophie was black-eyed, nervous, fluttering back and forth like a caged bird. She made motions as if she was about to walk into the library, then stepped back again.

'I died and I was about to leave, but then I found that poor person,' said Nana calmly, as Claire sat down next to her and started to get her trembling limbs under control. 'They don't know who they are, dear. They can't remember. They've lost themselves. I think they were murdered and thrown in an anonymous hole somewhere on this property. And I think – in fact, I am quite sure – that they were killed by someone in the family.'

'Um. Okay,' said Claire. 'That's… that feels like quite a bold take, if I'm honest, Nana. There are loads of ghosts in this house. A lot of people have died here. Including, you know…' Here she gestured awkwardly at Nana herself.

'Well, yes, but this person feels different, don't they?' Nana replied, and Claire nodded involuntarily; they did feel wronged, pained, lost. 'And they look… I don't know quite what you'd say, but they look like they're still—'

'Fresh,' completed Soph, who was still looking through the window. 'I think she's right. They're not very old, but they've lost who they are. They're barely aware of anything. It almost looks like they can't *think* even, and that only happens to, you know, violent deaths and unmarked burials, and things like that. I mean, isn't that why you never want to go near Marble Arch?'

Claire did a full body cringe. The Marble Arch corner of Hyde Park was near the site of Tyburn Tree, where public hangings had taken place for hundreds of years. Claire knew this partly because there was a little stone marker in the ground, partly because she was generally interested in history, and mostly because dozens of previously hanged ghosts wandered around there, joining the crowds at Speakers' Corner and yelling, shouting, trying to touch the living. But that wasn't the worst bit.

While they were generally the same age and personality as when they'd died, there was some elasticity to ghosts, especially how they looked. Some were wearing what they were buried in, rather than what they'd died in, some kept their gaping wounds and others were perfectly whole, but a very few were walking corpses. Sometimes people who died in violent or otherwise traumatic circumstances completely forgot who they were and so, in the absence of any other influence, they looked like what their body did. People would enjoy Marble Arch much less if they could see how many yellowing skeletons were sitting on the benches beside them.

And if the ghosts realized Claire could see them, they mobbed her, asking if she knew what was happening. Sometimes, if they couldn't speak any more, they simply screamed and shoved her. She never had any reply to give, so she avoided that whole area as much as possible. Newgate Street was also out, for similar reasons. And those skeletons were dry and dusty. The one in the library belonged to someone who was still... decomposing.

'They're not starting to go fuzzy, like old ghosts, either,' Sophie went on. 'They... feel new. Ish. About a year, I'd say.'

'That's why I think it was my family,' said Nana. 'Because not many events happen here in the autumn, you see. But there was a private party for my birthday this time last year, and there were a number of guests invited by the family, none of whom had met each other, or the family at large, before that weekend. And they all left suddenly, after a row. I never heard from any of them again, and I wonder if they did all manage to leave in the end... I think you should start there.'

'What d'you mean "you"? Do you mean *me*?' asked Claire. She was growing alarmed. 'What am I starting with?'

'You're the only one I can think of to help that poor soul, dear. Well, the pair of you. I must say, Sophie, it's a pleasure to be able to see you. You will help them, won't you? You'll find out who they are and set it right?'

'I mean... what? I can't...' Claire sputtered. 'We have to leave, Nana – they're organizing *your* funeral!'

'It'll be fine, my love,' said Nana, who was growing younger by the second. Her hair was falling in lustrous blonde waves down to her shoulders, her skin was fresh and wrinkle-free, and she gave a dazzling smile, with bright white teeth. 'Basher and Alex will help you, I expect. I'm fairly confident that those two are all right, you know. Say to Basher "Opal Fruits". And tell him... Say that I kept my word about the pink shepherdess incident. Until now. Right! Unfinished business over. Off I go.' And, just like that, she stood up. And was gone.

'Fuck,' said Claire. And then, 'Fuck. Shit. Fuckshit. What do we do now? Can we call the police?'

'Oh yeah, that'd be brilliant,' said Sophie, holding an invisible phone to her ear. "Hello, the cops? Yeah, I think this posh family murdered someone, because their dead nan told me so. No, I don't know who, or when, or how, or why. Also, please don't run my name through your files because we all know what will happen then." *Ohmigod.* You're so lucky I'm around to do the thinking for both of us.'

Claire swallowed. 'But I dunno, like... There isn't anything else to do, in that case. So, let's go?' She flapped her hands, frustrated and wanting to go home and eat chips.

'That doesn't feel right, either. That person needs help.'

'They've already been fucking murdered, so what are we supposed to do at this point? There's no way I can convince the family to let me stay here, when Nana has just died—'

'Oh, don't be so defeatist,' said Alex's voice. 'Just say that her ghost told you she buried a load of treasure in the garden. They'd be all over that.'

Claire looked round. She kept spinning stupidly on the spot, like a video game character when you've forgotten all the controls and are trying to figure them out.

'Look up.' Alex was leaning out of a second-floor window. They appeared to be smoking a joint again. 'I'll come down.'

'This is great,' said Sophie. 'Nana said Alex would help!'

It took a while for Alex to reappear, having sauntered outside and around the garden with the same urgency one would employ in getting a beer out of the cooler at a beach barbecue. Then Claire had to wait while they retrieved the stub of their joint from behind one ear – they had, Alex explained, put it out while they went through the house, in case Granny Clem saw – and relit it.

'So,' they said. 'What was all that about then? Who were you arguing with?'

'Er. Sophie. We, um, were talking to Nana,' said Claire.

Alex's eyebrow shot up. It was the one with the slits shaved into it, Claire noticed.

'Um. She's gone now. To be honest, Nana said... She said some stuff.'

'Interesting,' said Alex. They appeared to think of something and walked a little way out of the rose garden. 'Looks like we're alone,' they said, coming back. 'Spill 'em. Your guts, I mean.' They sat on the bench and patted the spot behind them, in such a mirror of Nana's gesture that Claire was quite taken aback.

So, with a lot of prodding and encouragement from Sophie, Claire told Alex what had happened, as honestly as possible – I met your nana's ghost, there is a terrifying skeleton haunting the library, and Nana is convinced that someone in the family murked a guest from last year's party – and hoped she wasn't going to get summarily thrown out.

Alex was quiet for a very long time. At one point they got up and, hands cupped around their face, peered through the window into the library. 'Yeah,' they said eventually, taking a heavy drag. 'That sounds about right.'

'What... really?'

'Yeah. I'm a practical person. Either you were actually talking to a ghost right now, or you're such a committed liar that you sometimes talk to yourself when you're alone in random places, to keep up appearances – and you obviously can't even commit to a hairstyle with any conviction.' They blew out a large plume of smoke as Claire baulked at such a casual death blow. 'And I do smoke a lot of weed, which helps me deal with unusual family news. I'm surprised it's taken this long for a potential murder to come up, to be honest. My dad in particular is a giant dickhole. And at what point does consistently voting for policies that defund social safety-nets and disproportionately punish the poor, disabled and queer not become a form of indirect murder?'

'Er... I don't know: at what point?'

'It was rhetorical, but, since you asked, I would say the answer is "very early on". Let's go and find Uncle Bash.'

Uncle Bash was holed up in his own guest bedroom near the kitchen. He and Alex made quite a strange pair, in comparison to the rest of the family. The others cut about in expensive shirts and neat cardigans and ironed trousers, but today Basher was in a faded and paint-spattered hoodie and Alex was in bright orange dungarees under a black faux-fur coat that crackled with static. It was like finding a gloomy pigeon and an angry raven hiding out amid a flock of fancy hens.

In any event, Basher was much harder to convince of the whole ghosts-and-familial-murder thing than Alex.

He still refused to entertain the idea that Sophie existed; even when she used Claire's energy to pull a lace doily a couple of inches along the top of the dresser, he said things like 'magnets' and 'fishing wire'.

'All right, this is a good one,' said Claire, after about forty-five minutes of attempting to persuade him. 'This one usually works. D'you have a pen? And a bit of paper or something?'

Basher produced a biro and a scrap of paper from the front pocket of his hoodie.

'Okay. Okay. I'm going to close my eyes. Alex can put their hands in front of my eyes even. And you write down whatever you want. Anything at all. I don't care. Doesn't matter. Literally anything. And then leave it face up on the table, so Soph can see. She can tell me what it says, and I won't even have to open my eyes.' Claire closed them, and after a moment felt Alex's hands cover them. She couldn't tell if their hands were very warm or if it had been too long since she'd touched a living person.

She could hear Basher sighing his assent. Then Sophie's reportage: 'He's scribbling to get the pen to work... Now he's licking the end of it. Okay... He's written, "Shall I compare thee to a summer's day? Thou art more lovely and more..." It looks like he's written "temperature"? His handwriting is terrible. God, what a loser.'

'"Temperate", not "temperature",' corrected Claire. 'Sophie says you've written the first two lines of Sonnet 18. Er... and that you're a loser with bad handwriting.'

Alex burst out laughing.

'You're a loser too, for knowing what sonnet that is,' said Sophie.

'I want another go,' said Basher. 'Keep your eyes closed.'

'He's doing the thing people do when they think they can win at this,' said Soph gleefully.

'She says you haven't written anything – you just pretended.'

'Now he's written PISS OFF, in big capital letters. I told you I liked these two, didn't I?'

Basher was still not convinced.

'Wait!' Claire cried, suddenly remembering. 'Nana said to tell you she always kept her word about, um... something. God, I can't remember. Nana was talking a lot and getting younger, and disappearing at the same time. It was a lot to take in.'

Soph wasn't helpful; she'd been paying too much attention to the skeleton at the time.

'Oh!' said Claire triumphantly. 'Oh, "Opal Fruits". That was something.'

At this, Basher narrowed his eyes. 'Opal Fruits were my favourite sweet when I was little. Nana took me to the beach once and I was scared I'd lose her, and she said if she sent anyone to find me, "Opal Fruits" was the codeword to know they were a friend, so I should trust them. But that is not actually proof that she spoke to you after she died, or that you have a dead best friend, is it? Just that you're very persuasive and people tell you things. You should think about joining the police.'

'I would literally, genuinely, prefer to also be dead,' said Claire, giving voice to the contradiction at the heart of her murder mystery obsession.

'Yes, *thank you*. It is a solid job with good career prospects. And a lot of camaraderie, not that you asked.' Basher flopped down to sit on the bed and stared at the floor. He seemed quite bitter, but Claire couldn't exactly tell what he was bitter about. He was very defensive about a job he had left some time ago.

'There are more things in heaven and earth, Horatio...' he murmured to himself.

'All right, well, we can sort out things viz. Uncle B believing in the paranormal later,' said Alex, with sudden briskness. 'I have other concerns.' They stomped over to the window, opened it and smoked a normal cigarette out of it, with brutal efficiency. Claire started to get nicotine pangs.

'Look, Uncle B, just give us your professional opinion – *ex*-professional opinion – on the case.'

'The case? The *case*? There isn't a case!' he replied, with an explosion of exasperation. 'Even if I accept that there has legitimately been a murder, which for the record I do not, where would you even start? Normally with a murder you have a body, which you use to work out who has died and how they were killed, yes? This isn't a whodunnit, it's a... a who*dead*it. And a *how*deadit. And a *when*deadit,' he finished somewhat lamely.

'Well, there's a finite pool of suspects, isn't there? No offence to you and your family, but the ghost is definitely a fairly recent one and it's haunting this house's library, so the killer is one of you. And there's also a finite pool of potential victims,' said Claire, who, if she was being honest, probably agreed with Basher more than she wanted to admit. But, crucially, she also did not particularly like Basher, so she was ready to solve the murder out of spite. 'Nana said she thought it was probably one of the guests at last year's party.'

'Good point,' said Alex. 'You two – three – make a list of everyone who was here last year. I'll go and sort it, so that Claire can stay.'

Under such direct instruction from a supremely self-possessed teenager, two hapless living millennials and one dead one couldn't help but do as they were told. Basher hunted around in a still-packed travel bag and produced a notebook. He seemed to be acting on instinct, in the absence of something else to do. He wrote a mercifully short list in what was indeed very messy handwriting:

- *Kevin*
- *Mattie*
- *Sami*
- *Michael*

'Okay, that's not too bad,' said Sophie. 'Let's work down the list, then… Who's Kevin?'

There followed about thirty seconds of silence, at the end of which Claire finally realized that Basher could not hear Sophie. 'All right, we're going to have to come up with some kind of system,' said Claire. 'I'm not used to you trying to have conversations with other people, Soph.'

'Are you talking to me?' said Basher.

'Jesus, it's like the Three fucking Stooges or something. Look, Sophie, if you *don't* want me to repeat you, tell me. Otherwise I'm going to parrot everything you say. All right? Clear? Basher, Sophie says could we please start with Kevin?'

'This is ridiculous. I do sort of commend you for taking your bit so seriously. But fine, the sooner we get this over with, the sooner I can get back to... oh, I don't know, mourning my nana.' He rubbed his face. His voice was not unlike his father's in its richness, but calmer and more even, as if he'd once been told that he was loud and had never forgotten it. 'Kevin was Figgy's boyfriend; they'd been together for about ten months, and she brought him down to meet us all for the first time. I felt a bit sorry for him. It was a trial-by-fire situation.'

Basher described Kevin as a wealthy mummy's boy who'd found himself on holiday in South America and had become a grubby Trustafarian type, who pretended he wanted to give up all his family money and become a monk, whilst simultaneously using said money to fund his extravagant international lifestyle.

'Mum absolutely hated him,' Basher summarized. 'Monty and Tris were pretty mean as well. I think it was a hostile environment for him. He and Figgy argued, broke up and Kevin left.' Basher shrugged, as if it was cut and dried.

'Nana said there was an argument. Was that it?'

'Sort of. It would be more accurate to say there were several cluster arguments that ended up coalescing into one giant, purple-spots-behind-the-eyes migraine of an argument.'

'Um. Like you quitting?' Claire asked, after a brief hesitation. Real detectives suspected everyone, right? Or they risked ending up in a Netflix documentary in twenty-five years' time, trying to explain why they didn't investigate the husband when, in hindsight, it was really obvious that he'd chopped up his wife's body and buried her under his new patio. *Yeah, yeah, Detective Handlebar McStetson, we've all heard 'people own massive knives for lots of reasons' before, but you still biffed it.*

Sophie had obviously had the same thought – well, not like exactly the same, but similar – because Claire could see her watching Basher carefully.

'Yes, that was one of them. Before you ask, it is none of your business. I don't want to talk about it.' He rubbed his eyes and looked tired again. 'Anyway. Suffice it to say that Mum and Dad were really upset when I told them I was packing the job in.'

'What d'you do now then?'

'Things. I've not really settled on anything. Copywriting, shifts in bars sometimes. Mostly I do cases as a private investigator, but it's all finding stolen bikes or trailing cheating boyfriends. Nothing exciting. Alex lives with me in Brighton, in a flat I bought when I was still gainfully employed.'

'Having a long, dark winter of the soul is affordable if you're from a family with money and property, huh?' said Claire, before she could stop herself.

'I would be affronted, but you are entirely correct.'

'What about this Kevin anyway?' asked Sophie. 'Let's get back to the murder. Is he definitely still alive?'

'I do not know. It's not like we kept in touch. Tris might know, I think he was friends with Kevin first – he may even have introduced him to Figgy. I cannot even remember his last name, I'm afraid.'

'Hmm. Okay. What about Mattie then? Who's he?'

'*She* is Mathilda. Mattie worked here for years, ever since I can remember. She started out helping at weekends and, over time, became the estate manager. She did most of the accounts and organizational things and was probably the most reliable adult around the place. I don't think Mum and Dad manage without her, to be honest.'

'What do you mean she "was"? What happened?' Claire asked.

At that moment Alex crashed back into the room, a small electrical storm that had managed to source a large paper flipchart from regions unknown.

'Right, Claire can stay. I told Grandad that we'd been talking and you were helping me realize that maybe I want to go to university and study PPE after all,' they said.

Sophie gave a loud bark of laughter. Alex swept the top of Basher's dresser clear and balanced their flipchart on top of it, snatched the list of victims and copied it out carefully in large letters.

'Where did you get to?' they asked.

'Basher told us about Kevin, and started introducing Mattie.'

'Is that all? Blimey.' Alex chewed the end of the biro and looked critically at the flipchart. They wrote 'POTENTIAL VICTIMS' as a heading, but started too enthusiastically, so it ended up looking like P O T E N TIALVICTIMS. They surveyed their work. 'Okay, maybe this isn't working. I know what we need to do,' they said.

'What?'

'A flashback. To Nana's birthday dinner a year ago. That would give you a better handle on things.'

'To do that, we are going to have to explain the entertainment last year,' said Basher. He was, for once, actually smiling.

'Oh *God*,' groaned Alex, 'there was entertainment. I think my brain had blocked that from my memory in self-defence.'

'We take it in turns to sort out some kind of act or band, or something. It was Mum's turn, and she did what we all do, which is book something shoddy and ill-advised at the last minute,' explained Basher. 'Present company, et cetera, and so on.'

'I guess it took the better part of a decade for the brief mainstream vogue of "fun" a cappella groups to filter through to her,' Alex continued. 'But she also tried to get a kind of Nana-friendly one, so' – and here they shuddered – 'so imagine, if you will, an a cappella group themed around the forties and fifties, mashed up with the hits of today. Except it was the hits of yesterday, because they were all sad thirty-year-olds like you two, wearing poodle skirts. Vera Lynn ft. Pitbull ft. Ludacris. It was a black hole formed of everything wrong with your generation. I could feel myself becoming an objectively worse person just by being there.'

'It was pretty bad,' admitted Basher. 'They were booked for the bigger party the next day, but for some reason Mum got them to perform the night before as well – sort of like your seance last night, but actually *during* dinner. It was... awkward, especially since everyone was already really tense anyway. Made all the bickering feel like part of a special musical episode on a TV show. They had some terrible name as well. You know, a pun.'

'It was The Clefs of Dover,' moaned Alex, pretending to half fall backwards against the wall, dangling their arms pathetically.

'After what happened, Mum told them the party the next day was cancelled, and I think they were offered rooms, but they elected to leave pretty quickly that night. For which I cannot blame them,' said Basher.

'God, it was like staring directly at the surface of the *sun*,' said Alex. They produced another regular cigarette, opened the window and sparked up, this time noticing the heat of Claire's stare. They were kind enough to share drags with her.

Thus, in between exhales out of the window, and with some clarification from Basher, Alex described that fateful evening.

4

Dinner and a Show

It was a dark and stormy night, both literally and in spirit. Most of the time the family just stayed in their part of the house, because most of the time there were a load of bankers or office admins charging around the grounds doing team-building exercises, or wedding guests being sick in the gardens and falling down the ha-ha. But for Nana's birthday and Christmas – also an intense and uncomfortable weekend affair – dinner was always in the proper dining room.

It was a weird choice, to be honest, because it was a massive room for only a dozen people. They could comfortably fit fifty in there for functions, so they always ended up all sitting down one end of the long table, and it looked and felt absurd. Whenever they ate in there the cutlery scrapes were really loud, like nails on a chalkboard, and combined with Tristan talking with his mouth full. Plus it was miles from the kitchen, so at least three people had to help carry things through and by the time everything was plated up, it had all gone a bit cold.

Anyway, that night dinner was roast beef with all the trimmings, which was Nana's favourite. There was a strawberry sponge cake with fresh cream. It was going to be lovely. Well, on paper, and if it had been a different family.

The weekend had already been more than usually complicated. Normally outside guests weren't invited to the family dinner. This time, however, there were several: Figgy had brought her well-meaning but annoying and somewhat noisome boyfriend Kevin; Sami, Basher's partner, had come along for moral support, but was seriously regretting it; and Tris and Monty had turned up with an accountant working with their firm, whose name was Michael. The last was a complete surprise.

Tensions were high going in, because of Clementine's constant needling of Kevin about his job, his future, his hair, and the way she kept smelling an odd smell whenever he was in the room, but couldn't quite place it. Monty was also doing this, but in a manner that wasn't so much needling as openly stabbing; and Tristan, who was often the family's equivalent of the shitty ratfink kid who stood behind the bully going 'yeah!', joined in because he copied whatever Monty did. The great irony, of course, was that this behaviour really only inspired a large amount of disdain from Monty, who would have been more impressed if Tristan struck out on his own. But Clem and Hugh were so absurdly protective of Tristan that Monty had got him a job at his firm to keep the peace. Tristan was just happy to slouch into whatever version of life other people made for him.

So by the time dinner rolled round, Kevin had endured thirty-six hours of basically undisguised insult; Figgy was embarrassed, but *by* him and not by her family's treatment *of* him; and they'd already had one argument about it themselves.

This dinner was the extravagant top hat on a day that had started out by pulling on the grim socks of a son revealing that he had quit the job his parents hated him having in the first place – seen by Clementine as a grievous insult to injury that caused a shouting match over breakfast. When Basher had first joined the police, his mother had been subjected to a deluge of jokes on the theme of 'PC Plod' (it was the sort of area where that passed for top bants). Clementine had, otherwise, produced two lawyers and a daughter who once had lunch with a Middleton, or at least had been in a room around midday at the same time as one, so a lower-waged son who didn't shop at John Lewis was a chink in the armour that Clementine's peers were quick to exploit.

At least when Basher became a detective it was good for casually bringing up at the checkout, when you ran into another mum whose son did something less noble and brave, like working in advertising. Morse was a detective, and it was good enough for him. The revelation that Basher did not feel noble and brave about his job, but in fact felt a bit of a shithouse and was having a personal and existential crisis – and didn't even do cryptic crosswords – was profoundly destabilizing for Clem and Hugh. At the same time, this was being revealed in front of *outsiders*, one of whom had arrived with Basher. Sami was supposed to be providing Basher with moral support, but she was already looking quite demoralized herself. The rest of the family had not really known how to treat her so far, and it was clear that Sami had taken on probably the most excruciating weekend of her life. At any rate, there had been tears in the scrambled egg.

It was also obvious that Mattie, who was usually such a brick, was being deeply weird with Clementine and Hugh. That weekend she had been either absent or hard to find for long periods of time, or locked away in the office.

Possibly even weirder was that Michael the accountant had, by dinnertime, disappeared entirely, after being driven into the village by Kevin and not returning. Monty was angry about this. Kevin claimed that he'd dropped him out past the station and Michael had said he quite wanted the walk back.

With hindsight, this was deeply suspicious and absurd, but by this point Kevin was so miserable around anyone other than Figgy that he couldn't be caught alone, and had avoided being interrogated further by Monty. In any case, Clementine was now also annoyed that they would have too many potatoes instead of too few, even though she had only acquired more potatoes specifically because Michael was to be joining them for dinner.

So, the events of the dinner played out like this:

Rain was sluicing down the windows in rivers. There was instantly an issue because at the time Alex was vegetarian and Clementine pretended to have forgotten this.

In fact she had been reminded several times in the run-up, and even the day before. She offered, by way of replacement for the portion of meat, a literal block of Cheddar from the deli over in town. Just a big lump of cheese.

'It's really very nice, darling,' she said. 'Quite as rich and lovely as beef, I'm sure.'

Alex elected to eat merely the vegetables and the other sides, and felt the cheese thing was a pretty passive-aggressive dig and that they were being deliberately excluded, especially when their dad started on about not knowing why they couldn't eat meat this one time, for God's sake.

'It's your great-grandmother's birthday, and the bloody thing is already dead anyway,' he said, throwing his phone down on the table with some force.

'Now, Monty darling. No phones at table!' said Clem, tapping his hand like a playful coquette.

'I don't mind at all, dear, of course,' said Nana to Alex, as the dishes of peas, carrots, cheesy leeks and cauliflower were passed down. 'It's just lovely to see you here at all. And I understand why you do it. It's marvellous all the things you can eat instead now. In my day it would have been quite impossible.'

'It's still your day now, Nana,' said Basher. 'And it definitely is today.'

'Here, here!' said Hugh automatically. He slapped the table a couple of times and it shook all the cutlery and glasses, making a jangling metallic sound.

'Yes, of course, Basher,' said Clementine, who had placed the impressive roast topside of beef in front of

Hugh. She pulled her chair in as Hugh started to carve. 'And everyone is quite free to make their own personal choices, aren't they?'

'Mum...' said Basher, in a warning tone.

'Well, they are!' said Clementine, defensive and innocent. 'People can make whatever choices they like, about what they eat or where they work or who they go out with.'

Kevin, whose body language was already screaming that he would rather be anywhere else in the entire world, pulled his chair closer to the table and glanced quickly in Monty's direction. He was prepared for a flanking attack.

'Look, can we just eat, please?' said Figgy, cutting Monty off at the pass.

They all turned to watch Hugh carving a row of thick slices, one after the other. He performed very well under the pressure of an audience.

The beef was, to give it its due, perfect. Juicy, exactly the right shade of pink inside, and with a crisp herby crust on the outside. Clementine could certainly cook very well, and everyone made the expected noises of approval.

'That looks lovely, Clementine,' said Sami. She had spent the weekend being polite to a fault, so as not to further tarnish Basher by association. Even for Sami's iron-clad self-control, the Wellington-Forges had been an unusual challenge.

'Thank you, poppet,' said Clementine. 'Do have some horseradish sauce, too.'

One advantage of a large dinner is that it occupies your mouth for quite a long time. This meant the family was given a good excuse not to speak while they hoofed down many pounds of protein and carbs, and vegetables covered in different forms of protein and carbs.

Tristan was obviously unable to read the room, though, so he kept making abortive attempts to start conversations that, if you didn't know Tris, you would assume were calculated to cause the most conflict. In fact, he was simply one of nature's oblivious blunderers.

'So, Basher, old chap,' he said jovially, 'what are you going to do for work now then? Any ideas?'

'Nope,' said Basher. 'None at all.' He shovelled a load of potato into his mouth in a carefree way.

'Well, that's good!' said Clementine. 'And I'm sure you'll be out on the street with nowhere to live soon.'

'Don't be silly, Mum, of course I won't. I have my flat.'

'And how are you supposed to pay the mortgage now? You'll end up back here, and it'll be *my* fault somehow!'

'Bash will be able to get quite a lot of consulting work, if he wants, Mrs Wellington-Forge,' Sami added quickly.

'You see? Please stop, Mum. I'm an adult.'

They lapsed into silence again.

'Could someone pass the gravy?' asked Tuppence.

'There's none left,' said Monty, in the middle of the act of pouring the last of it over his beef.

'Oh, well, not to worry,' she said, getting up. 'I'll make some more quickly. Do you have any Bisto, Clementine?'

Clementine explained that even though she knew Tuppence relied on the instant stuff, she herself always made gravy from scratch, but there might be some at the back of the cupboard somewhere.

Tristan cleared his throat and said, 'Good turnout for the birthday this year, eh, Nana?'

Nana twinkled at him. 'Yes, dear. It's lovely to see your shining, happy faces around this table, I must say.' Sometimes it seemed like she entertained herself by disguising sarcasm behind sweet-old-ladies-say-the-funniest-things-isms. It was hard to tell.

'Shame Mattie isn't here, though,' Tristan went on. 'Where *is* Mattie, Dad?'

Hugh said 'fired' at the same time as Clementine said 'sick'.

'Well, I mean,' said Hugh slowly, looking towards Clem for any obvious signs he was saying the wrong thing, 'she isn't here tonight because she's sick. But also we had to let her go.'

'What? Mattie? Why? When?' asked Basher.

'Well, it was a mutual decision,' said Clementine, taking a prim bite from a bit of carrot. 'We need to cut some costs, and Mattie wants to spend more time on watercolouring.'

'How odd,' said Nana, who had lost her twinkly, jovial air and replaced it with an expression of concern. 'You always used to say you couldn't run the place without her.'

'Anyway, Mum, Mattie has never done watercolouring in her fucking *life*,' said Basher, who was starting to do what he did in times of stress around his mother and revert to being a teenager. Sami laid a restraining hand on his arm.

'Don't swear, dear,' said Clem. There was a hint of a snap. 'For your information, Mattie has done a lot of seascapes of the Cornish coast.'

'As if you'd know, dahling brother – you barely ever come here,' said Figgy. 'Mattie could have had a whole seasonal collection in a gallery in town, for all *you'd* know.'

'Just because you're wholly unsatisfied with your life, *dah*ling, there's no need to take it out on me.'

'What's that supposed to mean?'

'We all know what that means,' said Monty.

'She's talking about Kevin,' chortled Tristan, at a normal volume.

'Oh, okay. Cheers then,' said Kevin.

'Anyway, at least I still have a job,' Figgy went on. She did not respond to the dig about her relationship but, crucially, did not deny it, either.

'Oh, please, showing your married mates different wallpaper swatches every three months and spending lunchtimes wanking around Soho doesn't count as a job.'

'Well, you'll need a new job soon, because I happen to know that Mummy and Daddy are cutting you off!'

'What?' Basher asked, turning to Clementine.

'Well, dear,' said Clementine, 'since you clearly don't value our opinions or feelings and are determined to be an independent man, that's what you'll be. But it's not a fitting subject for the dinner table.'

'Oh my God, you are absolutely unbelievable. Does my happiness come into it at all? What I want?'

'You do not know what you want,' said Clementine firmly, boring a hole into Basher with her stare.

Nana waited for a gap and sighed, loudly, which shut everyone up again, out of guilt. There was another long pause for eating.

'Not hard up, though, are you, Mum?' asked Tristan after a while, wheeling back towards yet another poor conversational choice and careening into it with the grace of a wacky clown-car with the doors falling off. 'Are you still thinking of selling up to those hotel types, Nana?'

Clementine slammed her fork down. 'Nana was never thinking of selling up, Tristan. It's off the table.'

'Oh, I'd like to keep it on the table, I'm afraid,' said Nana calmly. 'This one in particular is my birthday table, after all.'

'Well, we can talk about it tomorrow, when we're not in front of guests. Okay?'

'Yah, you should ask Michael for advice, Mum,' said Tristan, again lifting the fragile rabbit that was the evening in his big, clumsy hands for one last inadvertent throttling. 'He's a total genius at money stuff and the firm's accounts, and so on. I say, Monty, where *is* Michael? And what are we going to do about the thing he was talking about, with the irreg—'

'For Christ's sake, Tristan! What did Mum just say? Can you honestly not shut up for five fucking minutes?'

'I wasn't talking about the hotel types, I was talking about work—'

'Jesus, Tristan, I told you to stop, so stop! This is exactly why you're not allowed in any of the meetings any more.'

'All right, chaps, let's calm down a bit,' said Hugh.

'Yeah, Granny, please collect your large failsons,' added Alex helpfully. 'They're embarrassing the family in front of outsiders.'

Tristan was making the sort of face some young men do when they look like they want to cry, but direct it all inwards through a heroic effort at repression. It's the face of someone suffering from a cross between constipation and acute sunburn as they try to blow up a balloon.

'Yes, that is quite enough,' said Clementine. She put down her cutlery and clapped her hands together twice, like a nursery-school teacher calling the children to attention for storytime. 'We haven't even got to the cake yet! We don't want to make our guests feel uncomfortable.'

'You don't,' said a voice, 'want to make your guests feel uncomfortable? You *don't*. Want to make your *guests*. Feel *uncomfortable*.'

Every head swivelled. It was Kevin.

The air seemed to crystallize. Alex turned to look back at Basher and Sami whilst doing a comical gaping-mouth Muppet grin and could have sworn they were all moving in slow motion; Basher was starting to lean back in his chair as if he was accelerating in a fast car; and Sami was wide-eyed and shaking her head.

It was the moment before a natural disaster. A huge wave of insurmountable awkwardness – a sweeping, crushing tide of *Schadenfreude*, second-hand embarrassment and terrible arguing so acute as to be unbearable – was poised over them all. Alex imagined it suspended outside the dining-room windows, and in half a second it would sweep through them and lacerate them all with shards of glass.

It *almost* didn't happen.

Nana looked defeated. Clementine's knuckles were white. Figgy's mouth was half agape. Monty was reaching for his phone, so he could pretend to be disinterested in whatever happened next. Hugh didn't know where to look for guidance and was defaulting to his wine glass. And Kevin was giving off the same vibes as someone in a zombie movie who has definitely been bitten and is trying to conceal it from the rest of the group: red-eyed, pale-lipped, slightly green tinge to the skin. There was a moment when Alex thought Kevin was going to manage to swallow his next sentence.

But then:

'I'm sorry, Kevin, I'm not sure what you mean?' said Clem, with one of her bright, brittle smiles.

Three things happened at once. The first was that Kevin shouted, 'You're going to pretend to care about making us uncomfortable, when you've been making me miserable on purpose the whole weekend? Not good vibes!'

The second was that Basher pushed his chair back and jerked his head at Sami, whilst also making a move towards Nana.

The third was that Alex decided to make like a tree and fuck off, except they did it by *shoving* their chair backwards and sprinting towards the door with exaggerated limb-flailing.

Basher and Sami were slower, but Nana decided that she did actually want to leave as well, and asked Basher to take her to the kitchen for a cup of tea. They were coming round the head of the table with Nana in her wheelchair as Clementine said, 'Hugh! Are you going to let him speak to me like that?'

'Oh, er, sorry, Clem. Yes, Kevin old chap, that's not on, is it?' He stood up and grabbed the first items on hand, to gesture with for added emphasis, which meant he was waving around a carving knife and a half-full glass of red wine, which he was spilling over his chinos.

This caused Basher to stop and try and retrieve the knife from his father, and a small scuffle broke out.

As this was playing out, Figgy started shouting at Kevin in the approximate tones of someone who has turned up to ruin a wedding on an episode of *EastEnders*. It was rapidly devolving into full-on yelling on both sides and was the kind of argument where previous, very specific incidents were going to be brought up as ammunition. Indeed it was when Kevin said, 'Oh, wow, so this is going to be like that tea shop in Bath all over again, is it?' that Alex turned their head to look, yet continued in their forward momentum towards the dining-room door.

That is why they did not see it opening, as Tuppence finally returned to the room carrying a large jug of gravy.

At the last second Alex noticed their mum and managed to half turn away, whilst also throwing themself forward to try and get under the arm carrying the gravy. The result was that they barrelled into Tuppence's stomach and severely winded her.

Tuppence, of course, threw her hands forward without thinking, which meant that she chucked almost an entire jug of Bisto into the air.

It arced gracefully in a single shining sheet until its path was interrupted by Basher, Hugh and Clementine. All three of them were struggling over the carving knife and the glass of wine, and being suddenly doused in ribbons of slimy, hot meat-gunge did not improve the situation.

Either from all the added lubrication or from surprise at suddenly being more gravy than man, Hugh relinquished his grip on both glass and knife. The one smashed on the floor and stained the carpet, and the other flew into the air and landed point-down in the (antique) table with a cartoonish thud. It stood there, upright and wobbling, increasing the chaos tenfold with every wibble back and forth.

Alex started ministering to their mum and apologizing non-stop; Clementine was shrieking tearfully at Hugh about the table, while on her knees trying to mop up the red wine; Monty had seized the cover provided by everything going on to start hoarsely having a massive fucking go at Tristan; and Figgy was shouting at Kevin about the way he had looked at a woman in a bar in Islington one time.

Nana and Sami, who had narrowly avoided the en-gravying, both got a serious case of the giggles. Sami was snorting and chewing on her sleeve, and Nana had silent tears rolling down her cheeks.

Without warning, Clementine spun round to turn on them.

'Oh, I'm very fucking glad this is funny!' she hissed, hauling herself back up to her feet. 'I'm glad someone is enjoying this. This was supposed to be your birthday dinner, Mummy! And *you're* not even part of the family – how *dare* you?'

'Steady on, poppet,' rumbled Hugh. He was licking gravy off his hand in a kind of philosophical way.

'Oh, don't *you* dare start!' Clem shouted, wheeling back again. 'I'm working my fingers to the bone, keeping this place going, and what help are you? Don't think I haven't noticed money going missing. Or Mattie sneaking away in the middle of the day. What sort of grubby rendezvous are you having, eh?'

It's worth remembering at this point that, from the start of the evening, and indeed throughout the proceedings, about half a dozen thirty-year-olds in faux-retro fifties cardigans and Brylcreemed hair had been standing awkwardly to one side, singing.

They had, in complete fairness to them, carried on gamely in what must have been supremely weird circumstances, encouraged by stern looks from the woman with the tuning fork who was the lead White Clef. They'd only faltered a couple of times, notably during 'The Lambeth Walk' versus 'Walking on a Dream' by Empire of the Sun. The songs weren't natural partners at the best of times.

Although at this late stage they could barely be heard over everything, fully half of The Clefs of Dover were still struggling through a mashup of 'Boogie Woogie Bugle Boy' and 'Down With the Trumpets' (called, on their set list, 'Boogie Woogie Trumpet Bois').

Figgy let out a howl, grabbed a handful of cauliflower cheese from her plate and threw it at Kevin.

He ducked.

It hit the lead Clef squarely in the cleavage.

From then on, the evening broke apart a bit.

5

A Pint with the Lads

'Wow,' said Claire.

'Yeah. I mean, fucking hell,' added Sophie.

'I know it sounds weird, but honestly it's not that weird for *us*,' said Alex. They had closed the window and crawled over to the bed on all fours. Instead of sitting on it next to Basher, they lay full length on the floor with their head propped against it. 'A blowout like that happens pretty much every Christmas. It was just... extra blowout this time. It's not suspicious to us. It's Wednesday. Well, Saturday in this case. But I suppose at what point do you have to recognize your own dysfunction?'

'It is quite a lot of dysfunction,' said Basher, almost under his breath.

'We should debrief,' said Soph. 'Like, go over the evidence. Find clues.'

'Er. Soph wants to start looking for clues and stuff. But maybe we shouldn't do it here?'

'There isn't any evidence to find,' said Basher. 'There's no proof anything happened!'

Alex tapped the biro on their chin. 'Maybe. But if we talk about it enough, we'll find some. *Or*,' they added, catching Basher's expression, 'exhaust the possibility, and I'll get bored and stop talking about it. Anyway, Claire has a point about finding a secure location to talk. I bet you need a drink, don't you? I do.'

'You have me there, I admit. Fine, we can go to the pub. At least there, nobody – living or otherwise – can bother my parents. While they're *grieving*,' Basher added pointedly.

So they went to the pub. Claire was simply happy to leave the house and its unbearable atmosphere. The local turned out to be the one in Wilbourne Duces that Figgy had driven past the night before, red-brick but with a thatched roof and thick crown-glass panes in some of the windows. Claire knew, before they went inside, that it would have loads of horse brasses on the walls. There was a spaniel sitting outside, in such a grotesquely charming pose that it might as well have been an agency dog that was getting a decent day rate to flop on the steps. 'Yeah,' Claire imagined the dog saying, whilst smoking during a union-enforced break, 'this is a pretty good gig. I've got a spot as a patient on *Casualty* coming up, though.'

Where there would normally be a pub sign depicting a tree with a crown, or two men trying to strangle a swan or something, instead there hung a single plank painted red. This was because the pub was called the Red Line. Claire had been told this during the drive over, but had assumed Basher said the 'Red Lion', which she didn't think was an unfair assumption to make.

'Apparently,' Basher explained as they went inside, 'it was supposed to be called The Red Lion, but the very first sign-maker misheard, and so the Red Line it was for evermore. I do have reason to doubt this story, which is that it was definitely called The Red Lion up until it came under new management in the early noughties. It's a good story, though, and they do a decent shepherd's pie.'

'Ohmigod, is shepherd's pie the only thing people eat around here?' said Sophie. 'We should sit by a radiator or something. These two'll get cold, otherwise.'

They'd arrived for the lunchtime rush, but since it was in a village pub in the middle of nowhere, it wasn't hard to get a table of their choosing in a corner. It did indeed become a bit chilly, the longer Sophie sat there. Claire found that running an investigation from a pub came with a couple of distinct advantages, one being that you could work with a cheeky glass of wine.

The other was that the Red Line came with free Wi-Fi for patrons. Not only was the Wellington-Forges' home a dead spot for phones, but they were internet-free, apart from a wired connection in the estate office. It made the house a popular venue for a certain kind of wedding or corporate team-building event that used words like 'unplugged', but for everyone else it was really annoying. Alex noted that it made it very difficult to keep up with their social media pages, where they were building a decent following for their art and their costuming. They were now busily tapping away on an impossibly slim laptop.

'I know that story reveals that your family is even more

unsettling than the cousin-fuckers on *Downton Abbey*, but it does give us at least one interesting clue for murder,' said Soph.

'What d'you mean?' asked Claire. She had been so focused on the shouting and food-fight bits of the story that she'd almost forgotten to pay attention to the potential crime bit.

'Financial, obviously!' When Claire still looked blank, Sophie threw up her hands. 'Ohmigod, could you even tie your shoelaces without me? Clementine said something to Hugh about money going missing, first of all. And secondly, Tristan almost spilled the beans on something to do with irregularities that Michael found at the legal... the law... the lawyer-place. Where they build lawyers.'

'Legal firm?'

'Yeah. Michael's an accountant – he wouldn't have found irregularities in the ham sandwiches, would he?'

'That's actually a very good point,' said Alex.

'Er, can I add a "thirdly"?' said Claire. 'How fucking long did it take your mum to make instant gravy?'

'Yeah, now you mention it, she was gone for, like, forty-five minutes. Mum couldn't have killed anyone, though – she's not the type.'

'Everyone's the type,' said Claire very seriously. 'But it doesn't help much right now anyway. It's all, you know, hearsay.'

Basher looked up from ignoring the conversation, and concentrating on the menu, long enough to make a 'yeah, not bad' face.

'Can we tell if any of the potential victims are dead without digging up a body?' Soph asked. 'Wouldn't they have been reported missing?'

'Maybe. But Kevin might not be the easiest one to start with, actually,' Alex said, opening up Instagram, Facebook and a host of other social networking sites that Claire had heard of, but was not familiar with. 'Are you sure you can't remember his last name, Uncle B?'

'Neither can you,' pointed out Basher. 'Also, I would like it noted that I am not getting involved. I am here as a chaperone to make sure you don't do anything properly illegal whilst playing detective with a strange ghost-whisperer we don't know. Are you hungry? I'm hungry. They have pheasant stew on today.'

'Ah! I think this is him. Uncle Tris is following him on Insta,' said Alex, having been stymied by the lack of a last name for approximately twenty seconds. 'Hmm. It's an account specifically for a big trip he's doing around South America at the moment. His handle is 'NoPerryJustKevinGoesLarge. God, your generation is embarrassing. I think I would rather die than be one of you. Genuinely, Uncle B, I would kill myself, if I were you.'

'So that's three pheasant stews, O grateful one?' Basher said as he stood up, ignoring their dig. He went to order at the bar, shoulders hunched and hands in pockets.

Alex spun their laptop round to show Kevin's Instagram to Claire and Sophie. It was a lot of pictures of Kevin doing stuff like hiking through jungles, holding up a fish next to the local man who had clearly caught the fish himself, and smiling at children in traditional Peruvian clothes. Basher's description of Kevin had been accurate. He was white, good-looking and had several vaguely Celtic tattoos and lots of blue glass-bead jewellery. He probably had a COEXIST patch on his backpack.

'Last post was about three weeks ago. We can mark him down as a "probably not dead", I think,' said Alex, who had switched to working on a spreadsheet. They had indeed listed Kevin as Probably Not Dead.

'Sami isn't dead, either,' said Basher, returning to the table.

'I mean, you would say that,' said Claire. 'Surely if Sami was the victim, you'd be the most obvious suspect.'

'Sorry, you're right – I forgot that, out of all of us, you have the most crime-solving expertise.'

'I have *some*. Seances aren't easy, you know, there's a lot of investigation involved. Sort of. And I've watched all of *Murder Profile* at least three times,' she added, sounding as if she was joking, but secretly being serious. Basher snorted. Claire realized she was trying to impress him and made a mental note to catch herself next time.

'Don't be shitty, Uncle B,' said Alex, without looking up. 'Sami is actually alive – I've seen her since the party last year, too. A lot. We babysit for her.' They wrote Definitely Not Dead next to Sami.

'Yeah, unless you're both in on it,' said Claire.

'It would be good to talk to Sami, though,' said Sophie. 'Like, interviewing witnesses, yeah? Even the ones who haven't been murdered might remember things. We should, you know, reconstruct the weekend.'

Claire nodded without repeating aloud what Sophie had said, and made a further mental note to follow up on the Sami thing herself. If she'd learned anything from TV, it was that the person you least suspect is the person you should most suspect, and in this case that meant Basher and Alex. Even from a non pop-cultural angle, Basher at least made a good suspect. He had the know-how to commit and cover up a murder. She would simply need to figure out the motive – even if the victim wasn't Sami. Plus, it was probably a good idea to keep a healthy emotional distance from Basher and Alex, because eventually they would both decide they didn't want to talk to her ever again.

The pheasant stew arrived in large, steaming bowls. It was very hearty. There were dumplings and everything. Claire hadn't eaten any kind of game before. She discovered that pheasant tasted luxurious and meaty. Like chicken, but if hens voted Tory.

'Did anything else happen that weekend?' she asked, mouth full. 'You know, around the dinner?'

Alex and Basher paused and looked at each other, as if silently discussing how much dirty laundry they should air. Finally Alex shrugged.

'Not really. It was like this weekend, but with more shouting and less elderly-relative death. It was all those arguments, and then the non-family people left early and without properly saying goodbye, and the bigger gathering the next day was cancelled, out of embarrassment. You know, Uncle Bash argued with Granny and Grandad – Hugh and Clem, that is, not Nana – but Granny also argued with Figgy, and Figgy argued with Kevin. Oh, and Uncle Tris ruined a suit by falling over in it. I think that's less an event and more a metaphor for Uncle T's entire life, though. Like, at what point do you not realize that you are a walking stereotype? And the Mattie-quitting thing, but that happened sort of offscreen, from our point of view. I did see her a couple of times that weekend, though, and it looked like she had been crying.'

'Oh yeah. Um, what's the deal with all that then?'

'Mum would never admit it, but she can't properly run that place without Mattie. Like I said, Mattie was basically the estate manager, but Mum always said "housekeeper",' Basher explained, stabbing gloomily – which was how he did everything, Claire noticed – at a dumpling. 'It sounds ridiculous. I think Mum thought it was more proper for a big family to have a housekeeper. And in the summer Mattie's husband worked on the gardens a bit, so Mum could say the housekeeper was married to the groundskeeper. Very BBC costume drama, you know? Mattie had been working at the house for about twenty years, but packed it all in that weekend. Just quit. Or maybe got fired? Never got to the bottom of that really.'

Claire didn't point out that Basher's policy of non-involvement in the case wasn't standing up to much scrutiny. He obviously missed his job, or at least having some kind of defined purpose, even if he'd become disenchanted with being a policeman. Sophie was looking at him, an inscrutable expression on her face.

'My theory is that Granny shit-canned Mattie out of nowhere, because she thought she was having an affair with Grandad,' added Alex. They made a face at the thought of this.

'Yes, but you think that because it would be the most drama, not because you have evidence for it. I don't really believe that Dad would cheat on Mum,' said Basher. 'And Mattie was part of the family. She was always so nice to us. Like having an aunt. Loves kippers, as well. Was always making kedgeree. She lives around here somewhere. I was in the same school year as her son. In fact...' Basher said, craning his neck to look through the bar, 'I think that's her husband Alf over there.'

He pointed to a dour-looking man in a wax jacket and flat cap, the picture of a miserable country bloke. Alf was drinking a pint of ale, obviously, and was making a concerted effort not to look at anyone.

Sophie immediately said they should go over and talk to him, but before anyone could make a move in that direction, the door crashed open and in strode patriarch Hugh, flanked by two tall men in fashionable business suits. Hugh, in contrast, looked like he was dressed for some sort of obscure countryside Olympics. A tweed waistcoat and jacket strained over his tummy, which within seconds he was supplementing with a lager, and he wore matching three-quarter-length trousers that tucked into long maroon socks with fluffy garter-ties. Hugh, it was fair to say, did not have the legs for the ensemble. He noticed them at their table and shambled over.

'Been shooting then, Dad?' asked Basher.

'About to… about to. It was all arranged anyway, and I thought: why let the day go to waste? Nana would have wanted life to go on, you know, Basher,' he said, with an abrupt approximation of respectful sadness. 'Anyway, look at what the cat dragged in from London, eh? Chaps, meet Claire. This is m'dear little boy Monty,' he said, clapping a forty-something man on the shoulder proudly.

Monty was still handsome, with salt-and-pepper hair not unlike George Clooney's and a crisp white shirt and expensive watch, also not unlike George Clooney's. His eyes were as blue as his father's, but much more focused, and there was a smug twist to his mouth that Claire did not like. Alex seemed to have inherited more from their mother, thank goodness.

'Montgomery Wellington-Forge,' said Monty. 'Of Parker, Parker and Renwick. Figgy tells me we should be very pleased to meet you.'

Claire immediately filed this comment away for future petty seething, while Soph made a scoffing noise.

Monty was wearing a jewelled tie-pin that stood out against the relative sobriety of his suit: a silvery bar with three diamonds studded in it. The sort of thing you wear when you want to appear tasteful, but still want people to know that you have way more money than they have, or ever will. It glinted in the light.

Sophie was looking at it, too. 'There is absolutely no way he has enough money to spend on that, as the family in general can't afford to repaint their windows. Are you kidding me?'

Tristan, the youngest Wellington-Forge sibling, was pushed forward in his turn. He had a very square jaw, the same familial blue eyes and a messy blond pompadour that was, on closer inspection, actually rock-hard and frozen in place with product. Combined with the jaw, it gave the impression of a Lego-man from a Build Your Own Junior Lawyer playset.

'Yeah, hi. Tris,' he said, shaking Claire's hand and maintaining the grip for about five seconds longer than was comfortable. 'So. This is pretty weird, huh? You being here still. With old Nana dead in the back bedroom. Pretty awks. *Awkwarino.* Awkward city.'

He laughed nervously and sat down in Sophie's seat. She did not move, and the magic-eye picture effect of two people being in one place immediately began to make Claire's eyes water. Tristan would be feeling like he was sitting in an ice-bath, but, she was interested to see, he was trying his absolute best not to betray this fact by shivering or looking uncomfortable in any way. It was a losing battle.

'I'm not staying long,' Claire said. 'Er... my condolences, of course.'

'Yes, well, very sad, but it was a bit overdue, I suppose,' said Monty, who had not looked up from sending emails on his phone. 'I hear you're helping Alex sort their life out.

I don't suppose you can get them to move back in with their parents, where they ought to be.'

'Alex is nineteen, Claire, so they can actually live wherever they would like,' said Basher mildly, though he had flinched almost imperceptibly when Monty spoke.

'That's nonsense, and you know it. My child has been bloody kidnapped!' snapped Monty.

'Excuse me, can we not talk about me like I'm not here,' said Alex, trying to cut in between them, but they were interrupted by Hugh, who was not paying attention, saying, 'Jolly good, jolly good. Are you all right, Tris?'

'Your mother is worried sick all the time,' said Monty, cutting back across Hugh to acknowledge Alex.

'I'm totally fine, Dad,' whined Tristan as he squirmed in his seat.

'You look a bit cold, mate – we can switch places, you know.'

'Alex is perfectly safe with me, and I resent the suggestion that they are not.'

'He's always been a bit sensitive, ha-ha-ha, eh, Claire? Come on, Tris, I'll switch with you if you're chilly.'

'Still actually here – hello, has own opinions on their own life.'

'I'm not cold, Dad, I'm *fine*—'

At this point Tristan physically squirmed away from the jovial teasing of his father and/or the freezing-ghost aura, and tripped over a chair leg trying to stand up. He managed not to fall over completely, but staggered awkwardly, and two iPhones, his keys and a load of pens showered from his coat pockets.

'If you've broken another work phone, the firm isn't going to pay for it,' said Monty, without looking round. 'You're a bloody disgrace.'

'Er, no harm done, Monty. Sorry.' Tris scrambled to pick everything up, turning a bit pink.

Claire felt sorry for him. It was as if her mind had retconned Tristan staggering around, juggling all his possessions, going 'Wh-wh-wh-*whoooooah!*' until he sat in some jelly, even though that had not happened at all.

Hugh cleared his throat. 'Don't worry, Tris, Mum and I will get you a new one if anything is broken. Anyway, just seen Alf at the bar, chaps. I need to find out if he's going to be at the shoot this afternoon.'

Claire and Sophie exchanged a glance, and Sophie got up to follow Hugh as the three brothers began to exchange tense pleasantries.

'We're down here to see Mum,' said Monty. 'Brought the will down, and so on. But we'll probably have to leave again tomorrow.'

'Yeah, work is bloody *mental*, eh? Eh, Monty?'

Claire noted with some interest that Nana's will had apparently been drawn up by her own grandson, but she was distracted by Sophie, who was furiously waving her arms across the room. 'Look!' Sophie shouted. 'Look!'

Hugh and Alf were having a discussion in lowered voices, but it was obviously a *heated* discussion. Claire leaned back casually, so that she could see what happened next. Hugh, in what he clearly thought was a discreet way, reached into his pocket and pulled out a big folded wodge of cash. He passed it to Alf under the bar. Claire quickly returned to poking at her stew, as Hugh barked an awkward, too-loud fake laugh and returned to the table.

Sophie came back, too, and recounted what she'd overheard, talking in Claire's ear so that she could be heard over everyone else.

'Hugh said he wanted the "usual arrangement today", or something like that, and then that Alf guy said he wanted more, because people were watching and it was getting harder to avoid questions,' she told Claire, with conspiratorial glee. 'They weren't even talking that quietly.'

Claire choked on a hard bit of potato and Hugh slapped her genially on the back. She often found it weird, and inconvenient, to have to smile nicely at people while Sophie casually discussed secrets she had uncovered about them. Claire had to remember what she wasn't supposed to know, as well as acting like she didn't know it, and this was especially difficult in circumstances such as murder and investigatoring.

'Anyway,' Sophie went on, 'Hugh said it was the usual this time and he'd see about next time, but he wasn't happy about it. We need to talk to Alf, like, one hundred per cent. What if Alf hid the body and is being paid off?'

This was a good point. Alf was now industriously rolling cigarettes. He slipped one behind his ear, downed the last few dregs of his pint and headed outside. Claire waited for a few seconds, then waved her own lighter at the table apologetically and followed him.

Alf was holding the lead of the day rate glamour-spaniel and sucking aggressively on his rollie. He had acquired a cadre of similar men, all in various combinations of flat cap and wax jacket, and each in charge of a pink-tongued, shiny-coated dog. In a happy coincidence Claire discovered, checking for the fourth time since her last fag that morning, that her box of Marlboro Lights was empty. She approached the group cautiously.

'Er... sorry, mate. I'm out. Don't s'pose I could steal a fag off you?'

The men all stopped chatting and their heads swivelled. Alf looked at her with distaste. He was slightly unshaven and had the jowls of a very sad basset hound. Eventually he tutted and rolled his eyes, clearly unimpressed by a townie who couldn't even keep up her own supply of cigarettes, and fished out a roll-up for her, out of pity.

'Thanks, mate. So, er, you all mates with Hugh and the Wellington-Forges? I'm staying with them.'

'You're saying "mate" way too much for someone who never says "mate",' said Sophie.

Alf exchanged looks with the group. They seemed to come to a silent consensus to tolerate her, because he nodded curtly.

'I know 'em,' he said.

'Your wife, Mattie – someone said she used to work for them?'

'She did. Not any more.' There was no advance on the conversation.

Claire decided to try a different tack, and knelt down to say hello to the dog, which was very friendly. Especially in comparison to its owner.

'Nice dog you have. Beautiful! Hugh said you go on the, er, shoots?'

'We go picking up. Dipper never misses a bird.' There was some quiet pride there.

'Great. Yeah. Never been myself, but uh, I hear Hugh loves it. I guess he pays you to pick up for him?'

Soph whistled. 'Oooh, bold play from the rookie detective.'

To the surprise of both of them, there were a few snickers from the men. 'Yeah, Alf picks up for him all right,' said one.

'Always bags a bunch of birds, does Hugh,' said another.

'Mind you, there's a lot of that going around in that family, eh, Alf?'

'What d'you mean?' said Alf, eyes narrowing.

'Ah, nothing, don't get your arse in your hand.'

There was obviously some shared secret between them, but Claire couldn't think of a way to keep the conversation going. 'I, uh, I saw Hugh give you some money just now, that's all.'

'LOL! A bad follow-up, though; the opponent won't let her get away with that,' interjected Sophie, clearly enjoying herself far too much.

'Don't see how that's any of your business,' said Alf, turning to her as his eyes narrowed, if that were possible, even further.

'So, er, he *wasn't* paying you for picking up?'

'But the rookie hits back: fifteen all!' Sophie yelled.

'Stop fucking mixing metaphors – you're getting me confused!' Claire snapped back.

'What?' asked Alf, who was clearly thrown by this. The men shuffled their feet and gave Claire the disconcerted look that everyone gave her when she forgot to not talk to Sophie out loud.

'Not you. Ugh, bollocks! Sorry. Listen – just, how's your wife? Is she all right?'

'What? What do you mean by that? What have you heard? Who are you?' Alf was becoming not angry, but upset and embarrassed. Claire was surprised to see that his eyes were beginning to fill up a bit. She took a step away from him, as one of the men put an arm around his shoulders. 'Did one of you say something?' Alf asked, wheeling to look at them.

'No one said anything – I haven't heard anything about anyone. I'm sorry.' Claire felt guilty. She didn't yet have the hardened emotional carapace of a seasoned detective. Feelings had to be hurt in pursuit of the truth!

'Piss off and mind your own business,' Alf hissed, stomping away down the road. The other men, and their mismatched pack of dogs, headed off after him, giving Claire sour looks and insulting her loudly enough that she could hear every word.

She looked after them, still smoking Alf's cigarette. Sophie came and stood next to her. They stood in silence for a couple of minutes. Then 'Fumbled that one, didn't you?' said Soph, sucking air through her teeth.

6

Little Bones Go Snicker-Snack

The four of them had returned to the house. It wasn't too far a walk, really, although it was further than Claire would have liked and down a rough public right-of-way cut through the fields, in order to make a path as-the-crow-flies from the pub.

With Hugh off to his shoot and Monty and Tris having their own lunch at the pub, Alex told Claire that there was an opportunity to do a bit of snooping. 'If our lead is finances,' they said, 'we should have a rummage around the office, look through the business accounts, that sort of thing.'

But Basher was still not on board. He had ridiculous concerns about 'warrants' and 'chains of evidence', which were never mentioned on *Murder Profile* but which, Claire had to acknowledge, were quite important in real life.

'I'll keep him busy,' Alex whispered, letting Basher get a few steps ahead of them as the group walked across the gravel drive towards the house. 'You should be the one to look in the office, because it's the only place with a working computer. If you get caught, you can claim ignorance and say you didn't know you weren't allowed, and you wanted to check your email. Just don't let Uncle B catch you, okay? He is the CEO of overreacting, sometimes.' They patted Claire on the back to reassure her and called Basher back.

'So listen, Uncle B,' Alex said. 'I know you've gone all super-pig about it – all right, all right, it was a joke, calm down – but surely there's no harm in having a look around the general rooms and the big house? If we find anything, then we can leave it exactly where it is and not touch it; and if we don't find anything, then you can say you were right all along. And you love that.'

'Hmm,' said Basher. This was not a no. 'I suppose you can explore, if I supervise. Our fingerprints and hair are already all over most of the house anyway. But Claire can't touch anything. That would cross-contaminate.'

'Cross-contaminate *what*? How?' said Sophie. 'We haven't even been here before today. Ohmigod, he just doesn't like you.'

Claire might have imagined it, but she thought she saw Basher's cheeks colour a little when she relayed this.

'That's exactly why you would contaminate evidence – in the highly unlikely event of evidence ever being collected. And I am not trying to be mean. But you are not... you're a stranger. This is family,' he said.

'It doesn't matter,' replied Alex cheerfully. 'Claire can stay in the kitchen with Granny, right, C?'

'No, no,' said Basher. He clearly felt bad about the suggestion that he didn't like Claire. Which he probably didn't, but it might be weird to hear that said out loud to someone's face. 'I would not wish that on anyone. Look, would you stay in bits of the house where you've already been? Please? The library or your room, and so on. Please?'

Claire watched them walk away. She felt guilty that she was about to betray this trust. She had not yet mentioned that she and Sophie had seen Hugh paying off Alf. It was the only proper lead so far, a concrete thing suggesting that Hugh might have killed Mattie and covered it up – either by paying Alf to do the dirty work, or by paying Alf to keep quiet about something he saw. But it was a difficult thing to bring up. The enormity, the sheer ridiculousness of what they were doing, had become real to Claire, and she was trying to sit on that realization, like a large and uncomfortable egg, until she decided what to do with it. It was one thing to think you'd met a dead murder victim, and quite another to say to someone, 'Hey, I think your dad/grandad might have killed a woman and is paying her husband to keep quiet about her disappearance.'

'You should say something sooner rather than later,' Soph said. And she was probably right. But for now Claire was nervously chewing her thumb and looking at the door to the estate office.

Figgy was reportedly inconsolable and crying in her bedroom. Clementine was in the kitchen down the hallway. Dinner was going to be chicken soup, she'd told them all, and she was preparing the vegetables. Claire could hear the rhythmic chopping. But she didn't want to push her luck. She didn't really know how long it took to search a room. Was searching very labour-intensive? What about a 'fingertip search', compared to a general poking around?

She glanced again at the big oak door in front of her. It looked noisy. She opened it very, very slowly, as if she were unwrapping a sweet in the cinema or a sanitary towel in a public toilet. To her surprise, while it was heavy, the door opened quietly. She slipped inside, leaving it slightly ajar.

'Can you keep watch?' she asked Sophie.

'Ohmigod! No way. I want to see what they have in here, too.'

It was a small, oppressive room with no windows. There were a couple of filing cabinets, shelves full of storage binders, and a desk with a small office computer. There was also, as promised, a blinking router.

Claire gave a cursory rummage through the binders, but they were all physical receipts and she had no real idea what she was looking for. Then she tried the filing cabinets. 'You're looking under N for Nana, aren't you?' asked Soph.

'No,' said Claire indignantly, flicking quickly to M. At Sophie's suggestion, she checked under D for Du Lotte Hotels, the company that wanted to buy the building, and found a posh brochure dated the previous year, advertising winter breaks at a much nicer-looking estate than

The Cloisters. There was a business card for Mary Tyler, Head of New Developments, tucked into it. Someone had written, *'We can definitely help each other. Let's talk more!'* in biro and had added a mobile phone number. She showed Sophie.

'Ugh, those police shows have given you literally no common sense,' Sophie said. 'Sounds like someone from Du Lotte was in contact with a member of the family – or someone who was here last autumn, right?'

'Okay. So clearly selling the house was an issue around this time last year as well. But Nana wasn't involved in the day-to-day running of this place, was she? She didn't use this office. So someone else was doing some insider trading? They were sufficiently invested in the house being sold that they kept this contact info...'

'Yeah, maybe.'

'I bet it was Mattie. She used this office the most. What if they caught her – you know, passing info to the enemy?'

'Bit of a reach maybe, but I can see it,' said Sophie.

Claire was pleased with this success, but dithered about keeping the evidence, because she thought Basher would be cross. Sophie pointed out that she had already touched everything anyway, so in the end Claire took the business card and put back the brochure. Sophie rubbed her hands together: now, she indicated, they were cooking with some kind of flammable accelerant.

Next Claire went over to switch on the computer and establish her alibi for being in there. It was password-protected, obviously. She was already starting to get nervous, imagining that she could hear Basher's footsteps approaching every second.

'Try "password",' said Sophie. 'I bet you anything. There's no way Hugh would remember something more complicated.'

'Oh, come on, there's no way th— Oh, it worked.' Sophie was, Claire had to admit, still much better at this than she was.

'Fucking legend. Is there anything marked "our bad killing and how we done it"?'

Claire snorted, but she did have a look through the files in the vain hope that there was something obviously murdery. It seemed to be mostly more financial records and booking information, and she was not clever enough to understand if any of that was incriminating – although she harboured a vague suspicion that all rich people's finances were incriminating somehow. It did look as if the diary had started to thin out over the past year, or at least wasn't being kept as up to date. Perhaps Mattie had been more integral to the business than anyone – apart from Basher maybe – had realized.

Claire opened the email application and it automatically loaded the in-box. There wasn't anything suspicious in the recent emails, either, so she went back to around the same time last year. The Monday after the party weekend there was an email from Monty, from his firm's work address, that didn't have a subject line.

'Look!' she whispered. Sophie leaned over as Claire opened it. Her heart was genuinely racing. All it said was:

It's all under control. I told you not to use this
address. I'll call later.

Below it was the message to which it was replying:

We got an email from hmrc.they must have been
tipped off.if they investigate they will find out. w.hat
should I do now? dad

'Ohmigod. Fuuuucking hell,' said Sophie.

'It's not looking great for Hugh, is it?'

'No, I mean old people emailing. Surely he has to type
in his job?'

'He probably has a secretary or something,' said
Claire. She forwarded the email to herself, trying not
to think about how disappointed Basher would be, and
closed down the computer.

'You're going to be like that when you're old,' said
Soph, picking invisible spectral lint off her sleeve.

'You're six months older than me!'

'I am not! I haven't been since 2007. We've been
through this. I am for ever young and in my prime, while
you waste your life and become older and more decrepit
with every passing year.' Sophie's tone was breezy, but
she was avoiding eye contact. 'Talking about it gives me a
headache,' she said quickly.

'You can't get headaches,' said Claire absent-mindedly,
rattling one of the drawers on the desk.

'How would you know?'

'You don't have a head.'

'Do so,' said Sophie. She turned away and added, 'I'm just not sure where it is.'

Claire pressed her lips together. Even if nobody knew the specifics of what had happened to Sophie, everyone knew what the answer *probably* was, based on what usually happened to girls who went missing without a trace. It was on the long list of Stuff That Is Easier If We Just Don't Bring It Up, and Claire always got worried when Sophie showed signs of introspection. Who knew what she thought about at night, alone, unable to sleep, staring into the dark. Did she try to remember, or try to forget?

Claire attempted to concentrate on the task at hand. She pulled open a drawer and drew out a sheaf of letters, and a small, slim, bright blue notebook with what looked like a perfectly round blue eye on the front. She was about to open the plasticky cover, which felt like one of those waterproof ones you buy to protect the real cover, when suddenly she heard footsteps in the corridor outside. Instant panic – if Basher caught her with her hand in the cookie jar, he'd be very cross, and she did not like raised voices. She put the book back in the drawer and tried to shuffle the letters into the right order before stuffing them in as well. Before she had time to close the drawer, the door to the office swept open.

'Basher, sorry, I—' she started to say.

Clementine was standing there, staring at her. She paused, looking surprised, and then her features arranged themselves to convey a special kind of menacing kindness – politeness wielded like an ice-pick.

'Hello, sweetheart. Are you lost?' she asked.

'Uuuuuhhh,' replied Claire, who'd had just enough time to arrange herself with forced nonchalance in the office chair.

'Ohmigod, you sound like a confused cow. Say yes, for God's sake,' said Sophie.

'Hhhyes,' Claire finished finally. 'Sorry. I was. Um. Going to check my emails – someone said there was a computer in here, but of course the computer is password-protected, ha-ha. And then, um... my, um... sleeve got caught on the desk,' she babbled, trying to close the drawer as casually as possible.

'Of course. But I'm afraid there are lots of private documents in here,' said Clementine. She put her arm around Claire's shoulders to ferry her towards the door. 'Who was it who said you could come in here?'

'Aahhhmmm,' said Claire, who realized her voice had risen to an absurd pitch, 'I'm not *quite* sure.'

'Jesus *Christ*,' said Sophie. 'Sometimes I think that you're actually the dead one, I swear.'

'Of course you're not, dear,' said Clementine, with the sweetness of a sour lolly. 'Why don't you come and help me with the soup? I'm sure it will come to you.' She produced a key and locked the office door, before pulling Claire down the hall and depositing her at the kitchen table. 'You can finish peeling these potatoes for me,' she said.

Claire noted that it was not delivered as a question, and picked up the peeler.

Clementine resumed stripping the carcass of a roast chicken. She didn't look at Claire, but kept her eyes on the meat and bones as she pulled one from the other. Her fingers became covered with grease, but they didn't slip at all. Sometimes she would pick up a kitchen knife that had been worn to a thin strip by repeated sharpenings. The occasional *crack* as she drove it through a joint punctuated her speaking.

'Chicken soup is so comforting, isn't it? So restorative. I'm sure it'll cheer Figgy up.'

Crack.

'Of course, you don't have children, do you? I always think you can't understand until you do. Not really.'

Crack.

'You'd do anything for your children. Protect them from anything. From anyone.'

Cra-ack.

An entire drumstick was torn from the bird. The knife was raised and driven into the flesh again, and Claire found she was focusing on the only bit of nonsense she remembered from studying 'Jabberwocky' at school: 'One, two! And through and through / The vorpal blade went snicker-snack!' Round and round in her head it went, over and over again. *One, two! And through and through!*

Clementine dropped more cleaned bones onto the plate with little clatters. Then she picked up a wing and pulled it in two.

Snap-crick-crack. Snicker-snack!

She turned the bird over. Claire stared with ferocious intensity at the potatoes, and considered the combat potential of a vegetable peeler versus a knife. Sweat was breaking out on her forehead.

'Do you know what these bits are called, just here?' said Clementine, pointing out two little bits of dark meat near the leg.

Claire's top lip was also very sweaty. *One, two!*

'They're called the oysters. They're the most flavourful, best bit of meat. But you have to really dig them out.'

'*Ohmigod*. I think she's actually going to eat you,' said Sophie, visibly disturbed. 'Any second she's going to leap across the table and dig out *your* oysters.'

Claire did not find this helpful. *And through and through!*

Clementine drove a manicured nail into the offending bit of meat and began to winkle it out.

Claire watched with a growing dread. Clementine's fingers were slipping on the handle of the peeler, and Claire would give anything in the world for something to stop her getting the oysters out; something terrible was going to happen once she got the oysters out – please God, stop the oysters... *The vorpal blade went snicker-snack!*

Suddenly Basher and Alex exploded into the room. Claire yelped and jumped up, at the same time as Sophie exclaimed, 'Oh, thank fuck!'

Walking into the atmosphere in the kitchen must have

been like being hit in the face with a very awkward plank. Alex flinched.

'Everything all right?' said Basher, stepping forward to steal a bit of the chicken.

'Yes, darling, Claire was just helping me with the soup,' said Clementine brightly. 'Where have you two been? Would you like a cup of tea?'

The air returned to Claire's lungs. She breathed back out very slowly.

They all helped chop the remaining vegetables and put them in a large pot for later. Claire struggled. She stared at her hands and peeled potatoes, while Basher and Alex chatted with Clem. Her fingers trembled as the tide of adrenaline in her blood suddenly receded. She glanced up and caught Alex looking at her weirdly, so she looked down again.

'You been hanging out in the kitchen a while, Claire?' they said.

'Oh, Claire has been very helpful,' said Clementine. She tipped a handful of grains into the stock on the stove and smiled again. She maintained unblinking eye contact with Claire. 'A very busy little bee, aren't you, dear?'

'This woman is seriously fucked up,' said Sophie.

Claire finished the last potato with a sense of great relief. 'I'm just going to... um... please excuse me.' She ran back to her room, closed the door behind her and collapsed on her bed like a little girl hiding from a bully.

In a few moments Sophie walked in through the door. She mostly used doors like a normal person, unlike a lot of ghosts, even waiting for Claire to open them and go through first. It was either out of habit or wishful thinking. Sophie sat down on the other bed and whistled through her teeth, but otherwise didn't say anything.

After a while there was a knock on the door, followed by a tentative 'Hello?' in Basher's voice. Claire was lying with the pillow over her face, so she yelled an indistinct 'Come in.'

'Hello,' said Basher. 'What have you been up to, then? I take it, from Mum's behaviour, that you did not stick to our agreement.' He sounded more resigned than angry.

'Alex told us to look around the office, and then your mum did a one-woman performance of *The Texas Chicken Massacre* at me,' Claire replied, in a muffled voice. She pulled back half the pillow to see his reaction. It was surprisingly mild.

'I cannot say I approve at all, but I am quite tired, so please imagine that I shouted at you for looking through personal family documents and don't ever do it again, yes? Arguably, watching Mum debone a chicken carcass is punishment enough.' Basher paused and then, with a bit of a guilty tone, added, 'I suppose you didn't find anything, did you?'

'Yes. Well. Maybe. I don't know,' said Claire. 'Did you?'

'No. But the house is too big anyway. It's mostly dust sheets. And it's a whole year later. And I still do not think anything happened. But... well, I can see that you and Alex really are taking this seriously. I am not making fun of you by being sceptical.'

'Yeah, I know.' Claire sat up.

Basher was leaning against the dresser and the evening sun was cutting across his face. It made his grey eyes almost luminous and the soft blond stubble around his mouth stand out.

'What's that Alf guy like?' she asked, shaking off thoughts of Basher's face.

Basher shrugged. 'He's all right. He's a local old boy, hangs around with other local old boys, goes on shoots, takes good care of his dogs. Bit grumpy, but they all are. Indulges Dad, who is an abjectly terrible shot. Wouldn't have thought he was of any interest.'

'When did you last see Mattie?'

'Last year. What? I don't come here often,' he went on, rubbing his face. Claire noticed he did that a lot, enough for it to be a habit. 'Claire, Mattie is probably fine. If she had gone missing, someone would have noticed. I am sure she got a much better job somewhere else. "Nothing will come of nothing",' he added, a little sadly.

'Tell him – go on. About Alf,' said Sophie, who was now picking at her nails.

'Soph... listened to your dad talking to Alf in the pub. And I saw him hand over a load of money. I asked him – Alf – about it.'

'Ah, the direct approach. And?'

'He told me to piss off.'

'You shock me. When you say "a load of money", what do you mean?'

'It was a bunch of twenties folded in half. Like you see

drug dealers passing around on TV, in the detective shows Claire watches,' said Sophie. 'Except neither of them was wearing a cool leather jacket.'

'Hmm. I'm pretty sure Alf isn't the type to have a sideline in gak. And my dad isn't the type to take it.' He paused. 'Now, if you'd said *Tris*...'

'Well, what *was* the money for then, if not to keep Alf quiet about something? Plus, I found this business card from Du Lotte, which makes it look like someone was in cahoots with them. Clearly Nana wasn't the only one interested in the house sale – so who else was?' She passed the business card to Basher, who frowned and turned it over in his hands. '*And* I saw an email from your dad to Monty from last year saying, like, HMRC had been tipped off and were going to investigate the family finances, tax owed and that sort of thing, so what should he do? And Monty was like "Don't contact me at this address". What if that's something to do with Michael?'

Basher scratched his chin. His fingers rasped a little across the stubble. 'Ye-e-e-s, well, reading people's private correspondence is getting into dicey territory, legally speaking...' he said. But he sounded and looked worried.

'It was an accident,' said Sophie tartly. 'Claire was trying to read her own email and your dad's just opened, right? Anyway she's not a police officer, so no harm, no foul.'

'Hmm. I'll be honest. When I asked, I wasn't expecting that you'd uncovered evidence of actual wrongdoing.' Basher started to pace back and forth, as much as was possible, and kept pushing the sleeves of his hoodie up to his elbows and then pulling them back down again. He suddenly wheeled back to face her. 'We're getting back to the point where I find it hard to trust you, I'm afraid. It feels more likely you've made this up. You could have written on this card yourself, and everything else is just your testimony.'

Claire shrugged. She was used to mistrust. 'You can go and look at the emails yourself. Anyway, why would I bother making it up?'

'To get me on board with this *investigation*,' said Basher, dropping heavy air-quotes around the word.

'I thought you weren't making fun of me?'

'This is not me making fun of you, this is me being catty.'

'Bit full of yourself. Anyway, if I wanted that, I'd have made up an email saying, "Dear son, hope nobody finds out how we totally killed someone!"'

'All right – maybe you want to blackmail my parents for money.'

'In which case, why did I tell you about it?'

Basher looked at the ceiling. He was weighing up the logic of her arguments, which Claire thought was pretty bang on, in fairness. She pressed home her advantage. 'Look, I know you don't believe I can see dead people, but you don't have to think I'm the worst person in the entire world. Something weird *is* going on here, and I can tell you want to find out what.'

'No comment,' he replied, flashing a shy smile. '*But* as you pointed out, that email is not evidence of murder, is it? At the end of the day, you've caught my dad emailing his son and paying for something cash in hand.'

'I dunno. It seemed more shady than that. And your mum is very aggressive about the correct way to strip a chicken.'

'Even so. That would not, as we used to say, hold up in court. Although... *arguably* Monty could say that email is confidential, under legal-advice privilege, since he is the family lawyer and Dad asked him what to do. So why wouldn't he want the email to go to his Parker, Parker and Renwick address? Unless the firm itself was exposed somehow...' He put his hand over his mouth and lapsed into silence, eyes unfocused, deep in thought. 'Bollocks! I'm going to have to get a bit involved, aren't I? This isn't playtime for teenagers any more.'

'Hmf. See? Shady,' said Claire.

'Just don't call the police yet, please. Creative accounting and tax-free business aren't in the same league as murder. This is probably all some huge misunderstanding, so I would like to learn more before you waste police resources. In the meantime, I will continue to assume you are being genuine. It is nice to be nice.'

'Honestly, weirdo, you should be relieved he doesn't want to involve the police,' said Sophie. She was picking at her nails again. 'You know. Because of Essex.'

'Er, yeah, okay,' Claire said to Basher, without repeating Sophie's comments this time. 'We'll see what we can find out for ourselves, first. That seems fair. What's their last name, by the way? Mattie and Alf, I mean,' Claire asked.

'I don't know,' Basher said and had the decency to look embarrassed. 'She was always just Mattie to me.'

Claire flopped back onto the bed. 'God, what is it with you lot and surnames?'

'All right, calm down. Easy enough to find out.'

'That's not the point – you should know already. You know, you're not so different from the rest of your family,' she snapped, with sudden bitterness. She wasn't entirely sure where it came from.

'Right, okay. Pleasure talking, as ever,' Basher said. And he left.

Claire lay in silence and stared at the ceiling. Out of nowhere her eyes started prickling, so then she felt annoyed and sad at the same time.

'You totally deserved that,' said Sophie. 'He was actually being quite nice.'

'Piss off.' Claire put the pillow back over her head. It was all quite confusing and upsetting. Was the theory that Hugh had killed Mattie? Or that Hugh and Monty killed Mattie together and were hiding it from Clementine? In which case, emailing about it on a shared business address was a bit stupid. But then Hugh did have that sort of energy... But Mattie couldn't force them to sell the house, so why would they need to kill her in the first place? But if it wasn't that, what *was* Hugh giving out shady backhanders for? But, but, but... The possibilities were endless.

Clementine had been very angry to catch Claire in the office, so maybe she was in on it as well. Maybe it hadn't been to do with the house at all, and instead Mattie really had been having an affair with Hugh, and Clementine had caught them at it and stabbed Mattie to death in an instant rage? Then Hugh would be shamed into helping her cover it up.

Claire yelled into the pillow and immediately regretted it, because the cover got into her mouth and made her tongue all dry and fluffy.

'Maybe we should just go,' she said, suddenly feeling very tired.

'What?' Sophie exclaimed. 'You're giving up already? It's been less than a fucking day! What about Nana? You promised! What if she gets un-unfinished businessed and comes back?'

'I can't, Sophie. This is already too weird, and I'm tired,' said Claire. 'Also, I don't want to be turned into soup.'

'*Ohmigod*. When the going gets tough, the tough piss off back to London, eh? Come on, this is the only interesting thing that's happened in the last... three years, at least. Could be worse. *You're* not dead or anything.'

'You never complain.'

Sophie sighed and flopped weightless on the bed, on top of and/or through Claire's feet. Claire wiggled her toes as they became frigid, like standing in an icy stream while wearing welly boots. She pulled her knees up out of the way.

'I miss KFC,' said Sophie eventually, staring at nothing.

'Not nice expensive restaurant food, or home-made cake or anything?'

'Or creepy chicken soup? Nah. Mum was a shit cook. I miss KFC chicken. And McDonald's. Remember going to see *Finding Nemo* at the shopping centre and getting a burger afterwards?'

'Yeah. You snogged Martin Yates during the film and said he'd been drinking Fanta, and it got Fanta all on your face.'

'Yeah. *Finding Dory* wasn't anywhere near as good as *Finding Nemo*.' They'd gone to see that at the cinema too, but it hadn't been the same – not only because Soph had been dead for almost a decade by that point.

'Yeah.'

'Is KFC shit now?'

'I could lie, but no. It's still great. If you can forget that the chickens live miserable, painful lives, which, when I'm hungover, I choose to do.'

'I don't mind being like this exactly,' said Soph suddenly. 'It's just that it gets boring sometimes. You're the only person who ever talks to me normally, but Alex actually believes I exist and says stuff to me. And Basher does too, as long as he isn't thinking about it.'

'You're the only person who ever talks to *me*,' said Claire, feeling a bit like a teenager who thinks her best friend is being stolen.

'*I'm* fucking *dead*, whereas you're too boring and weird for everyone else. I don't have a choice.'

'You are literally the thing that makes me weird, though, if we're honest.'

Soph looked a bit sad, which was alarming in itself, because she normally wavered between impassivity and happy flippancy. Claire was so used to her being around that they didn't talk much these days about the fact that she was dead. She'd first turned up just a week after she'd gone missing, suddenly standing next to Claire at her own candlelight vigil, her shining eyes reflecting the flames. It had been a shock. Soph had always liked to make an entrance. But now it was simply how things were.

And yet sometimes, like now, they skirted around huge and improbable questions – like what would happen to Sophie when Claire eventually kicked the proverbial bucket, or how Sophie had died in the first place. In fact Claire was one of only three people who even knew for sure that Sophie was dead. Technically speaking, to the world at large Sophie was still a missing person. And maybe it was nice for the girls they'd gone to school with to be able to move on and forget, and in another five years say something like, 'I think a girl I was at school with ran away from home actually' at a dinner party. And maybe it was nice for Soph's family to cling to the possibility that she was still alive. But Claire didn't have either of those options. She knew Sophie was dead and had been dead for years, and in fact was often reminded of this by the second person who knew: Sophie herself.

The third person who knew what had happened to Sophie was whoever had killed her.

To Claire, Sophie was still vibrant and present, and she laughed and tossed her hair and complained about every-thing and nothing just as she always had, but to the rest of the world she had become a footnote. A sad, unsolved mystery from decades earlier, a girl who disappeared one weekend and whose ghost couldn't even remember what happened to her, and who occasionally had threads posted about her on very specific bits of Reddit.

And she could never eat fast food again.

'Can we please stay and figure this out? You're the one who's supposed to like detective stuff,' said Soph, after a long silence.

'Yeah, okay. We'll stay a bit longer. But we have to start doing it in a way that makes sense or I'll properly throw a wobbler. All we did today was go to the pub, and I feel like I'm on the verge of a breakdown.'

'Okay.'

'Also, you need to stop saying so much while I am doing interrogations. It really throws me off.'

'I won't stop saying *everything*,' Soph replied, raising an eyebrow. 'We're like good cop, shit cop. If I didn't give you ideas, it'd just be shit cop.'

Claire didn't think this was entirely fair; it was not, after all, Sophie who had the bedrock of knowledge from repeat-watching fifteen series of *Murder Profile*. She wanted to object, but decided to have a prohibitively hot shower to try and pep herself up a bit instead. She sat down in the bottom of the bathtub and played the game where if you angle your arm right, it looks like you can control water.

She sat in there for almost forty-five minutes and thought about Sophie. Maybe her life, her death and their life/death together was something they should talk about.

In fact it was almost 100 per cent certainly something they should talk about. But since they were both each other's sole moral support, and had been for years, neither of them had the emotional maturity to do so properly. It'd be like the blind leading the blind, if everyone involved was also a weird cross between a thirty-plus-year-old and a teenage girl.

In the early days Sophie had tried to remember what had happened. The entire day of her disappearance was a blank for her, but there were odd things. As a ghost she had, for example, a new, intense but inexplicable hatred of the scent of thyme. In the beginning she and Claire had hypothesized, come up with theories, even called the murderer 'The Third Man' and imagined that he sounded like Orson Welles and made a joke of it. But there was nothing to follow up on. It stopped being funny the more years passed, the longer Sophie couldn't remember, the older she didn't get. Eventually they stopped talking about it at all.

It wasn't as if there were relationship therapists who specialized in counselling for you and your dead best friend (though there were, they had discovered, when Claire had mentioned Sophie's appearance to her parents early on, therapists who specialized in it as an adjacent issue, but that had not been helpful). So. Probably best to not go round, or through, but to head in a different direction and avoid the whole thing entirely. Yes. Good.

Claire mentally updated her own version of the list that so far comprised their entire investigation:

Victims

- *Kevin, Figgy's ex – Probably Not Dead*
- *Mattie the housekeeper – Possibly Dead*
- *Michael the accountant – also Possibly Dead and needs investigatoring*
- *Sami – Possibly Dead: not taking anyone's word for it yet*

It seemed to be a definite fact that someone on the inside had been passing info to the predatory hotel chain, and someone (maybe the same someone) had passed info to the tax office on some shady finances the family were involved in. Either of these represented a decent motive for murder, but the someone in question could have been any of the four potential victims.

Claire almost added a sub-category of Suspicious Persons, but decided this was futile, given that it would include basically everyone she had met so far. She did, however, put Clementine in a special column in part of her brain marked 'What the Fuck?', alongside such characters as 'old manager who made me try and get condoms from the NHS walk-in centre because she didn't want to pay for them and she'd heard teenagers could get them for free' and 'man who stroked the back of my neck at the zebra crossing that one time'.

Organizing her thoughts went some way to making her feel less anxious, so she was a lot happier after she dried off and got dressed again, pulling a fresh T-shirt and pants out of her bag. The plastic baggy holding Sophie's pink hair-clip fell onto the floor and she tipped the clip out onto her palm. It was technically a piece of evidence; the police had found a couple of the hair-clips that Sophie had been wearing in the search for her, but since they were generic hair accessories and there wasn't any trace evidence on them, after a while they'd been returned to Soph's mum. Claire had stolen one from her house when she was about twenty-one, on the urging of some dark impulse (Soph telling her to do it), and she felt bad about it. But it was a physical connection to Sophie. It was here, and it was still on Sophie. A dead object. Claire didn't think about how this meant that Sophie must have been wearing it when she died.

Instead of putting it back in its bag, she rolled it between her fingers and rubbed her thumb against it, like a worry bead. She put it in her pocket. It made her feel a bit better.

'It's good that chickens don't get unfinished business,' she said when she eventually came back into the room. 'Or *I'd* never eat KFC, either.'

But Sophie wasn't there.

Claire stuck her head out into the corridor, but there was no sign of Sophie. She took a few experimental steps towards the kitchen and felt a little jangle on the invisible line in the opposite direction. It took her past the office into the main house.

She slipped as quietly as possible through the corridors, because she was pre-guilty about being somewhere she shouldn't. She was aware this was exactly the wrong attitude to have, though. Behaving like you belong everywhere was, after all, how families like the Wellington-Forges moved through life – but Claire didn't have it in her. Sophie did. She had been able to go wherever she liked even before she was able to go, ghostly, wherever she liked.

Claire shuffled down a long corridor and passed a big, dark-wood door that she opened to peep through. It was a dining room, as large and imposing as the library, and it seemed even bigger because the long dining-room table only took up a comparative sliver at the centre of the room. It was an island in an ocean of varnished wooden floor. Claire's feet echoed very loudly as she crossed it. She looked at the ceiling and spun round, keeping her eyes fixed on the chandelier. There was a lot of impressive moulding and gold paint, but on second glance you could see the cracks in the facade. The room didn't smell of polish, it smelled of dust. The paint on the moulding was starting to peel and the chandelier was catching cobwebs. She looked down at the table and saw a deep scratch in it that had been repaired with wood putty. She ran her thumb over it to feel the slight break in the smooth surface.

She kept going and realized that Sophie was back in the library just before she got there herself. It looked very different at this time of day. The sun was setting, so the bars of light thrown across the room were bright gold instead of the silver-grey cast by the moon the night before. Claire could still feel the wrongness, the tinny taste of sadness, which was even more pronounced now that she knew it was there, and why. But the room was definitely empty, apart from Sophie stepping impatiently from foot to foot in the middle of the room.

'Ohmigod, finally,' said Sophie.

'What are you doing here?' hissed Claire.

'I saw them!'

'Who?'

'*Them*. The fucking skeleton! I got bored waiting for you and went out into the corridor and they were at the other end. They looked at me and then turned round and staggered off here again. It felt like... I dunno, they didn't exactly beckon, but I think somehow they know we're here. I think they're trying to help.'

'Well, where are they now?'

'They came over to these shelves here,' said Sophie, pointing at a section of the library near the fireplace. 'They were sort of scratching, like trying to get through the books, and then they fell forward, into the shelf. And they were gone.'

Claire was secretly pleased. She wasn't sure she was up to another face-to-skull meeting. Although the library was at least a long way from Clementine and the kitchen.

'Hello?' she ventured, for the look of the thing. But anyone who might have been listening stayed as silent as the – a-ha-ha – grave.

Sophie was looking at the books on the shelves. 'It's all classics. Shakespeare and Dickens, and big old encyclopaedias and what-have-you. I bet nobody has ever read any of them.'

'Smells nice, though,' said Claire, inhaling the deep, musty scent of old leather and paper.

'Maybe there's a secret passage,' said Sophie. 'Quick! Pull out some of the books – maybe one is a lever. Like on TV.'

That seemed a bit unlikely to Claire, but she knew from long experience that it was better to comply with Sophie's requests, unless you really enjoyed constant humming or singing, or loud shouting while you tried to speak to anyone else. She began pulling out some of the books.

'Ooh! This one – do this one!' Sophie was pointing at a slim volume on the bottom shelf. It was conspicuously blue, in a row of red volumes.

Claire crouched down and tipped her head to one side to read the spine. '*The Old Man and the Sea*,' she said. 'All right, here goes.'

She reached out and hooked the top of the book with a finger. There was a slight resistance as she tugged it. Her heart jumped and she locked eyes with Sophie. She pulled again, harder. The book slid out, top first.

Nothing happened. Claire pulled again and *The Old Man and the Sea* came out all the way. It was a normal book.

'This is stupid. Can't you just look through the books?' Claire asked.

'Oh, yeah. Sorry. I'm so used to you having to turn on the TV for me that sometimes I still forget I can do stuff you can't.' Soph leaned forward and stuck her head and shoulders through the shelves. 'There's definitely something back here,' she called, slightly muffled. 'It's dark but... there's a space. Like a cupboard. Maybe it's a pope-hole?'

'A what? Ohh, I see. It's "priest-hole", but well remembered. It's weird, I wouldn't have thought this building was old enough to have one.'

Priest-holes were little hideaways built into posh Catholic houses during the 1500s and 1600s, when Catholicism was outlawed. If anyone came to check that you weren't doing any naughty Masses, you could bundle yer priest into the secret cupboard in the staircase. *No, sir, only good clean Protestants here!* Priest-holes were one of Claire's favourite oddities of history. It seemed such a high-effort, impractical solution to a problem that it circled right back round to practical. And, of course, it was evidence that laws really only apply to poor people. For rich people, most laws are just minor inconveniences. If they wanted to keep going to Mass, they could simply build a secret church in their own house.

Claire looked down and saw an ornate section of carved leaf on the bottom of the shelf, right where it met the stone of the fireplace. It was clearly not a solid part of the shelving. She pushed it in, and there was a click and the shelf popped out. She pulled it open: over and through Sophie.

'Well, you were sort of right, I suppose. But I mean, it's a bit obvious, isn't it?' she said, unimpressed.

'It's not going to fox your average Popefinder-General for long, nah,' agreed Sophie.

132

The space behind the not-particularly-secret door was about the same size as a small wardrobe. Claire got in. It smelled a bit musty, and had the odd, empty aroma of a room that is cold all the time. There were cobwebs on the walls, but they were old and abandoned – no flies in here. There were smears of dried mud on the wall, too, down near the floor. Claire picked at a flaky bit sticking out, and it turned out to be an ancient dead leaf. She bent down and saw there was actually quite a *lot* of mud, on the wall and on the floor too, and some faint water stains. She pointed it out to Sophie, but as soon as Sophie stepped inside the space she did a kind of full-body spasm, like she had cringed with every muscle at once.

'Eesh,' she said, after recovering, 'can't you feel that? The body was in here. For definite.'

Claire shut her eyes, but she didn't feel a thing. 'How do you know?'

'I dunno. I just do.'

'Ah, like one of those specially trained dogs, is it?'

'Well, it's not like I had loads of experience being dead before I died. I don't know how it works. But they walked into the shelves here, and their body was definitely kept in here at some point. I think that's why they're still hanging around in the library.'

Claire brushed the mud some more. It was very dry, so it had been there a while, but she didn't know if you could, like, forensically date a dirt smear. It made sense, though.

'I believe you. But *why*? The mud would have had to come from outside. Why would you kill someone outside, drag them *inside* and then move them again? If you're already outside, might as well chuck 'em in a ditch or cover 'em with leaves or something.'

'Hmm. Maybe. Claustrophobic yet?'

'It's quite roomy, actually,' Claire said. 'Compares favourably with our flat.'

'Bet it starts to feel poky with the door shut, though,' said Sophie.

Claire reached out and pulled the door to, leaving it cracked a little. Yeah, probably wouldn't be heaps of fun to be stuck in here for a couple of days, while a bunch of humourless Protestants with a hard-on for persecuting Catholics tore up the floorboards outside.

Something sparkled and caught her eye. The concentrated line of light from the door was falling on something shiny, stuck between the floorboards. Claire crouched down and worked it loose; it was a little fake crystal button, the sort you might find on the cardigan of a nice mum.

Just as she stood to examine it more closely, there was a creak as someone pushed the door closed and the locking mechanism clicked into place. She was plunged into total darkness.

Claire sighed, and waited.

There was a blast of cold as Sophie came in. One advantage of having an invisible friend is that it's quite hard for anyone to punk you. 'It's Tristan and Monty, obviously. You all right?'

'Mmm.' Claire knocked on the door. 'Hell-oo? Could you, um… let me out please? I can't see anything.'

There was no response, apart from some obvious snickering. 'Look, I, erm… I know it's you, Tristan. If you let me out now, it'll save a lot of time, won't it? Please?'

'Maybe you should pretend to be scared instead. It's what they want,' Sophie suggested.

'I have some self-respect, thank you,' muttered Claire.

'Coulda fooled me. Have you considered that you might have been trapped in a box by some vicious killers?'

Claire had not. She pressed an ear to the door, but couldn't hear anything. Logically she knew that eventually someone else would come back into the library, but at a more emotional level she knew in that moment that the entire family were cold-blooded murderers and they would enjoy hearing her pathetic scratches on the door as she starved to death while they ate dinner.

She smacked on the door with the flat of her hand. 'Hello?'

Silence.

She hammered with a bit more urgency. 'I would like to come out now, please. Come on!'

After a few more seconds there was a click-clack and the shelf popped open. Monty was standing a little behind Tristan, still typing away on his phone as if he was above it all, but with a thin-lipped little smile. Claire was 100 per cent sure that Monty had told Tristan to do it, like the school bully giving himself plausible deniability. He turned sideways, and the diamonds on his tie-pin flashed in the sunlight, so brightly it made Claire wince and look away. He couldn't have done that on purpose, could he? Surely nobody was able to weaponize jewellery.

Tristan, meanwhile, was doubled over with exaggerated laughter. 'Oh my God – your face! God, you were so scared! "I can't see anything",' he said, choking back tears. 'Oh my God, you're so freaked out: look at you! Ha-ha-ha. Oh, blimey. Don't worry, it opens from the inside too. You were totally safe the whole time.'

Claire stared at him. 'Yes,' she said. 'Yes, sure – you really got me there. Top. Top banter. Bants. Whatever.'

Monty was looking at her curiously, as if he were a scientist and a single-celled life form with no intelligence had just waved up at him through his magnifying glass. Claire didn't like it.

'You like exploring our house by yourself, don't you?' he said suddenly.

'I think Clem has been telling tales after cookery class,' said Sophie, who was trying to get a look at Monty's phone.

'Yep, well. I'm a student, I mean I was; I was a history student. Not any more, obviously. But I like... old... things.'

Monty raised an eyebrow. 'Is that so? So what can you tell me about our priest-hole then?'

'Ohmigod, this guy is gatekeeping *history*,' said Soph.

Claire drew in a deep breath. 'Actually I don't think it's real. I think it was put in later as a curiosity, because the house isn't old enough, it's really badly hidden and it's way too big,' she said, in one nervous breath out again.

'Oh, wow!' exclaimed Tris. 'Monters, she's bang on. You're bang on.'

'Shut the fuck up, Tris.'

Tristan flinched a little, like he'd been slapped.

'Anyway,' said Claire, who once again felt like her skull was shrinking at the profoundly weird, confrontational awfulness of this family. 'I am going to go. Back to my room now. Thank you. Goodbye.'

She sidled out of the room. Something about Monty made her feel like she was in the wrong, or on the back foot. She suspected he'd learned it from his mother.

But in her hand she clutched her sparkly little trophy, like an Olympic gold medal. If she found out who this belonged to, then maybe she would find the murderer.

7

Soup for the Soul

Quite a lot had already happened that day, so they had returned to their bedroom to catalogue their new evidence. Claire and Sophie sat and stared at the button. It was on the bedside table under the reading lamp, which Claire had turned on. The button looked like it was being interrogated in an interview room. Claire stared it down. She felt sure it knew something. It was definitely a clue. A Clue.

'We don't know if it's a clue, weirdo,' said Sophie. 'It's probably Clementine's. She could have dropped it there yesterday while cleaning, for all we know.'

'Maybe. But it didn't look like anyone had cleaned in there for ages. It was still muddy, remember? Ugh, what kind of person builds a fake priest-hole into their house?' Claire continued to glare at the button. If this was *Murder Profile*, it would have an initial carved into it or something. Or represent the killer's mother or possibly sister (who died tragically young).

'All right, what do we know so far?' asked Claire.

'Fuck all. LOL.'

'No, seriously, come on. Your memory is better than mine. I want to write some of this down.'

'Ugh, okay. So we know that someone died here, in distress, about a year ago. Let's assume it was one of our two suspected victims from Nana's birthday party – excluding Kevin, for reasons of Instagram.'

'Three victims. I don't think we should trust Basher and Alex completely, so I'm keeping Sami on the list. Basher is an ex-cop, and he's still really sore on that subject.'

'Okay. So, it's Mattie the housekeeper, Michael the accountant or Sami, Basher's ex. We don't know how they were killed, but we do know their body was stored in the priest-hole in the library for some time.'

'Right,' said Claire. She was scribbling bullet points on an envelope she'd found in her bag. 'And that they might have been muddy when they went in there. And at some point someone was in that priest-hole in clothes with buttons like this.'

'But it might not have been at the same time, or related to the murder. Not everything is a clue.'

'Lots of things are a clue. Like all the money stuff – the HMRC stuff, and someone having dirty dealings with the hotel chain.'

'None of that implicates anyone definitively, though,' said Sophie. 'The tax thing is more likely to have been Michael, but he wouldn't have been involved with Du Lotte. That's more of a Mattie move, surely? It doesn't make sense for them to have been done by the same person, but it's also a big coincidence if they weren't. It's very annoying.'

'I know, but I think getting all my thoughts in order is helping,' said Claire. 'I think there's definitely a financial element to this crime.' She started writing more, making links between different potential killers and victims.

Sophie got bored almost immediately. She got up, stretched and went to look out of the window.

'Hey, stop looking at that, weirdo,' she said suddenly, and beckoned Claire to the window. 'Ted's skulking around down there... What is he doing?'

Soph leaned over and called down to him. 'Ho! Ted! What're you up to, eh?'

'I'm sampling the pain and emotion of the human condition, Miss Sophie, such as is now beyond my reach, and has been for many a year,' came the faint, haughty response.

'You're doing *what*?'

'I'm listening to Miss Figgy having a good old cry.'

'Oh. I'd forgotten about her.'

While in keeping with Ted's vaguely voyeuristic attitude in general, this sort of thing wasn't an unknown phenomenon among the dead. A lot of ghosts were drawn to humans experiencing strong emotions, of all kinds. Claire got the impression that a ghost's emotions gradually slipped away, the longer they were dead, until feelings were memories of feelings. Eventually, unless they put in the effort, they became vague foggy wraiths, floating aimlessly, lost.

And so a lot of them were drawn to fits of emotion in the living, treating sadness or elation like the aftershave of a middle-aged man in an enclosed space: a thing that could be soaked in, experienced vicariously, even if you weren't wearing it yourself. And, indeed, whether you wanted to or not.

Sophie wasn't like that – at least not yet. She was going through a phase of wanting to watch exclusively romantic comedies, but that could have been for unrelated reasons (like, for example, being tired of repeat viewings of *Murder Profile*). In fact Soph was presently flapping her arms and making big eyes at Claire.

'Come on. Let's go and talk to Figgy. Now's our chance!'

'Why am I the one who has to do everything? I'm not even bloody related to her. Can't we make Basher or Alex do it?'

'That's exactly why you have to do it. The others would be, you know, compromised as witnesses if they had to give evidence.'

'Whatever,' Claire grumbled. 'The things I do for you.'

'This isn't for me, weirdo. This is for Nana. And justice. And the American way.'

'Oh, fuck off.'

Claire's reluctance was mainly because she didn't particularly like Figgy, as Sophie well knew. It didn't stem *just* from Claire's innate prejudice against people of Figgy's make and model – which had mostly developed after university anyway – but from the fact that Figgy had always been kind of a self-involved dick. They'd not been close friends, but they'd been in the same halls of residence in first year and had friends in common, so they ended up orbiting each other quite a lot.

Claire remembered her as very similar to how she was now, only slightly less grown. If Figgy in the present was a horse, past Figgy was a foal. A bit gangly, but still a long-legged, sleek creature that could be described, by some, as elegant or even majestic. She studied PPE, but without any evident interest in any of the letters, and was always exactly the right amount of fun and drank exactly enough.

Claire drank a lot when she was at university. Sophie's existence gave her a profound sense of otherness, but also a kind of selfish bravado. Nothing would happen to her, probably, and even if it did she had a witness who could tell her everything that had occurred. So, ignoring Sophie's protestations, Claire tried to reinvent herself and leave behind the strange, pale girl who had to have loads of therapy after her best friend disappeared. Who lost most of her other friends. Who started talking to herself, or to thin air. She would be the fun one.

She poured burning hot spirits down her throat and threw them up again before the end of the night. She fell asleep nestled in the cold hollow next to the toilet. She had one-night stands that she regretted almost before she'd even had them. Claire still associated university less with her classes and more with the taste of sambuca and the dizzy embarrassment of retching in an alley at 7 a.m., as middle-aged women in sensible jeans did the school run mere feet away. It was, in the end, a failure, because Sophie was always still there. And, really, Claire didn't want her gone. Sophie teased Claire when she was falling over drunk, but pressed her cold hands to Claire's face when she cried in confusion at 3 a.m. Sophie stood in the hallway yelling if Claire ever brought someone back to her room, but Sophie was the one who was always there in the morning.

Next to people like Figgy, who seemed so poised at the age of nineteen, Claire felt like a hot, lumpen fool full of bile. Everyone at uni had quite liked Figgy, because she made you feel very important. Even Claire, the first time they'd met (at a party, at Claire's house). Figgy had been luminously happy to be introduced. But this facade began to fall away the next time they met and the time after that, and every time after that, because each time Figgy would reintroduce herself as if they had never met before. And this cast other things, like Figgy casually opening *your* fridge and getting out *your* bottle of white wine, in a different light. Once, Claire had told her that her dress looked nice, and Figgy had thanked her. Then, ten minutes later, someone else had said her dress looked nice, and Figgy had said, 'Oh my *goodness*, thank you – do you know you're the first person to have said so?' Claire wasn't sure if Figgy had a problem with her specifically or was a bellend in general, but either way she wasn't impressed.

Figgy had even reintroduced herself when she, and a group of old uni friends, had spotted Claire in the queue at a Pret a Manger a few weeks ago. It had prompted Sophie to yell, 'God, not this awful bitch again!' and Claire spent the whole conversation with an openly mutinous expression – at least until Figgy mentioned offering her a job...

'We can't just... turn up, can we?' Claire said to Sophie now. 'I need to have a reason to show up at Figgy's room, I can't arrive going, "I know your entire family are here, but I thought *I* would be best at comforting you in your grief." That's not normal.'

'I dunno – posh people have weird ideas about normal behaviour, don't they?'

Claire thought about it, and then very tentatively made her way back to the kitchen. Basher and Alex were sitting on one side of the table, with Hugh and Clem on the other. They were eating soup.

'Hello,' said Basher. He raised an eyebrow. 'We were just wondering if you were hungry.'

'Um. Yes. But I thought, if you hadn't taken any to Figgy yet...' Claire trailed off, unsure of herself.

'Not bad, weirdo,' said Soph. 'Good impulse.'

'Oh, that's a great idea!' Alex leapt up from the table. 'Here, I'll get a tray...'

Soon Claire and Sophie were following Alex back through the house. They stalked the halls with a tray loaded with bowls of chicken soup, like a high-fashion goth version of Meals on Wheels. It was a great opportunity, they pointed out, 'to strike Kevin off the list for good'. They were clearly still as enthusiastic about the project as Sophie.

They knocked cautiously on Figgy's bedroom door and entered in response to a quavering 'Yes...?'

It was obviously Figgy's room through childhood and teenagedom, and now occasionally adulthood, when she came home. It was a decent size and, unlike Claire's B&B-esque room, showed some personality. The walls were lilac, and there were shelves of trophies for different sports, rosettes for events that Claire suspected involved horses, and several teddies staring at her with blank black eyes.

Figgy was lying full-length across her double bed, one foot tucked under the opposite knee, one arm cast across her face, and a tissue clutched to her breast in the other hand. Claire felt slightly resentful: Figgy was justifiably in mourning and could not be grudged this, and yet if you had told her that Figgy had carefully arranged herself thus before her visitors entered, she would not have called you a liar. It was unfair for someone to be annoying whilst living through legitimate sadness, because Claire wasn't allowed to be annoyed by it, which was even more annoying, and it locked her in an ouroboros of being a shitty person.

'Oh, darlings,' said Figgy, with a weak sniffle. 'It's too awful. Too, too awful.'

'I know,' said Alex, not unkindly. Claire distanced herself from her uncharitable thoughts, and reminded herself again that their nana had actually died an actual day ago, and they were all actually related. Sophie was right; this was all probably way less taxing for Claire than it was for anyone else.

Figgy sat up to take her bowl of soup on the tray and tucked her feet under herself. Alex took a seat at a small desk. The desk chair had once had part of a cheap feather boa glued around the backrest for decoration, and the remains flopped limply off one side. Claire, after an awkward look around, knelt on the floor.

They all sat in silence, slurping their soup. Life here, reflected Claire, seemed to revolve around meals. Pies, soups, stews. The only other activities people got to do were ultimately for sourcing food. Where are we going? Off to have lunch. When will we be back? In time for tea. All hearty, home-cooked stuff. It was probably quite annoying for Sophie and her KFC cravings.

Also, it was all very good. Maybe Clementine's recipes were a closely guarded secret, or maybe they were a stolen secret. Maybe she had a folder of pages torn out of *Good Housekeeping*, but told everyone they were all old family recipes handed down over generations. Maybe that's what she was hiding in the office. Perhaps she would go on a murderous rampage to protect them.

'I feel a bit better after that,' said Figgy eventually, as her spoon scraped the bottom of the bowl.

'Yeah, I'm pretty sure if I had to live on my own I would die,' said Alex. 'Like, I would either starve to death or die from overdosing on pasta and mini-doughnuts. Those are literally the only two options.'

'You should get one of those delivery boxes – the ones that send you all the ingredients and instructions,' said

Figgy. 'I had a fully organic one from Abel & Cole. And another that sends me fresh flowers every month.'

'Yeah, I'll get on that right after I start shopping exclusively at Harrods and buy a three-bed flat in Soho,' said Alex, who did not miss a beat from taking a photo of their long nails. They were bright pink with shimmery stripes of gold glitter on each ring fingernail, and Alex had correctly spotted that they looked good against the backdrop of a lilac wall.

Figgy made a non-committal scolding noise, and asked Claire what she thought about the soup.

'Oh, yeah, er, it's really good,' she said, taken off-guard. Soph rolled her eyes at her again and went to peer at the trophies and bookshelves.

'Hmm... Showjumping and gymkhana stuff, nothing really interesting there.' She ran a finger slowly and critically along the spines of the books. '*The Seven Habits of Highly Effective Dickheads*... a lot of stuff on the "Men Are from One Planet, Women Are from a Second, Different Planet" theme... a few romances, but modern girls having it all, rather than bodice-rippers. Those ones are all really worn, so she likes them. But there's one here about meditation – ooh, and a copy of *Chicken Soup for the Soul* – and the spines aren't even cracked.'

Claire processed this information: self-help, romantic troubles, insecurity, pretending to like new age shit. The latter felt firmly in Kevin territory.

'Have you read *Chicken Soup for the Soul*?' asked Claire.

'I have a copy here, but I haven't read it,' said Figgy. 'It... well, it was a present from Kevin, my ex. He gave it to me last year.'

Alex gave Claire an undisguised look of astonishment; without knowing that Sophie was the mastermind, it must have looked like Claire had made a frankly amazing shot.

'Oh, sorry,' said Claire. 'I didn't mean to rake anything up. I just thought, I think I read a post by, er... er, Gwyneth Paltrow? It's supposed to be very uplifting in... in sad and stressful times.'

It was not, at least in Claire's mind, totally implausible that Gwyneth Paltrow would post about *Chicken Soup for the Soul*, presumably as part of a long ramble on Instagram where she also talked about steam-cleaning her fanny to get rid of bad auras (Special Fanny Steam Water only $700, plus international shipping). Figgy did not appear to notice anything untoward about it, either, because she nodded.

'Yes, you're right, darling. Maybe I'll read some tonight. Just, gosh, I don't know if I can start thinking about Kevin right now, too! A loss is a loss, my therapist says, and a break-up can hurt as much as any other.'

'That actually sounds quite sensible,' said Sophie thoughtfully. 'It would be something she learned from someone else.'

'Did you really like him, Aunt F?' asked Alex.

'I did. I thought I did. Kevin was this amazing free spirit, you know? Sometimes he would turn to me and say something like, "Figgy, let's go to *Barcelona* and eat chicken croquettes in the shadow of the *Sagrada Família*",' she said, getting a dreamy look in her eyes. Figgy hit the accents on 'Barcelona' and 'Sagrada Família' like a 2 a.m. pisshead swinging enthusiastically for a bouncer, and it made Soph laugh.

'Go on,' she encouraged Claire. 'See if you can get her to say "chorizo" next. Ten points.'

Claire pressed her lips together to stop herself laughing. She realized that Figgy really hadn't changed since university.

Alex had, without Claire noticing, produced a small embroidery hoop from somewhere in the depths of their jacket, and was working on a circle of mixed autumn leaves and fruits surrounding the word 'OOOF', in exquisite cursive script. They said, in a carefully neutral tone, that they remembered Kevin having a lot of opinions about various religions and global cultures. 'And also,' they added, in a slightly less neutral tone, 'gender. He used the phrase "sacred feminine" several times.'

'Oh yes,' said Figgy, absent-mindedly, still in Barcelona. 'Yes, he's brilliant. And so switched on about social issues, you know? But it would never have worked between us long-term. Mummy was right.'

Claire murmured 'star-crossed lovers' sympathetically, and Figgy nodded with approval. 'What happened?' Claire asked, pushing on.

'Well, we'd been together for a few months, and I got on really well with his folks – Sue and Jeremy, lovely little cottage in South Withemswall – so I decided to bring him to Nana's party to properly get to know everyone. But Monty was being so rude, asking about Kevin's job prospects. He couldn't understand that someone like Kevin doesn't *care* about job prospects. He cares about what's really *important* in life. He calls them M&Ms – memories and moments.'

'Yeah, I remember him using that phrase at lunch on the Saturday, too' said Alex. 'I think he made an impression.'

'He did on Mummy, anyway. At least according to Kevin. He said she pulled him aside after that and told him outright he wasn't good enough for me. I was quite shocked, I told him I couldn't *believe* she would do a thing like that.'

'I can,' said Claire out loud, at exactly the same time as Sophie. 'Er, I mean… Clementine, your mum, she's very protective of you all, isn't she?'

'Yes, but I'm totally my own person, and she respects that,' said Figgy. 'So then things were a bit sour between me and Kevin for the whole day, and after dinner, when we'd all had a bit of wine and… Well, Kevin said he wasn't going to stick around if my family were going to treat him like that, and I'd better decide if I was going to choose them or him.'

Claire asked what she had done, with appropriately bated breath.

'I chose my family, of course!' said Figgy. 'Kevin was so… He was different, you see. I think Mummy was surprised. But I do miss him.'

'Did you ever see him again?'

'Oh no. I stormed off to, well, this room. All tears at bedtime, I was *quite* emotional. Kevin went to the garden to try to centre himself, but I don't think he came back to bed even. The next morning he was gone. Someone said he'd headed off early to the station.'

Alex made significant eye contact with Claire. 'I didn't see him either,' they said.

'Well, he does text me every so often still, so we chat, but he's moving around a lot,' said Figgy.

'Oh!' blurted out Claire. 'You do?'

'Not often,' said Figgy defensively. 'Kevin's in South America now. It was just hard to cut him out. He's so open – not like anyone else I know. But he broke up with me via text, did I tell you that?' She scrolled back on her phone and passed it over:

17.37 Sorry Figgy Pud, this is all really unfun. Ur fam are fucking mean & pretty bad vibes

17.37 i dont like whats been happening. have to get out of here tbh.

17.37 we can talk properly when im home

Claire agreed that Kevin was clearly a massive prick, which is what you're supposed to do in these situations. She quickly scrolled to the most recent messages. One from Kevin said, *'goin 2 colombia next. still no plans 2 come bak sry bby.'* Then there was a big list of messages from Figgy asking how he was, and if he was safe and okay, and what he was up to that night, and if he'd met anyone nice, dot-dot-dot, pregnant question mark. Then an hour later Kevin responded '*ttyl*'.

'Oh, Aunty F,' said Alex, glancing at the messages and grimacing. 'You should really disconnect entirely if you want to move on. Self-care, you know? At what point do you become responsible for your own happiness? As soon as possible, if you ask me.' They bit off the thread they were using and then looked at it. 'Shouldn't have done that – that's screwed it right up,' they burbled to themself.

'You're right, Alex, I'll delete all of it!' cried Figgy suddenly.

'Oh no, fuck, don't do that,' said Claire, panicking as she saw critical and important evidence being flushed down the digi-drain. Figgy looked at her weirdly. 'I mean, er... if you don't know where you've come from, you can't know where you're going.'

They left Figgy nodding sagely and thanking them for visiting, with the mournful largesse of Queen Victoria in her widow's garb.

'Okay, let's go back to the kitchen,' said Alex. 'It's the only properly warm room in this ancient, single-glazed nightmare of a building.'

Claire hesitated. 'Er, I sort of would rather. Not go back there. Or something. I don't know.'

'What? Why?'

'Normally I would be making fun of her for this, but actually I agree with her,' Sophie said, and Claire repeated this backup of her position. 'She has fair reasons to feel safer alone.'

Alex rolled their eyes. 'Right, so obviously for some big weird reason you're keeping private, you are terrified of going anywhere near anyone else right now, is that it?' They were towing Claire down the hall with one hand, and fishing a cigarette out of another internal pocket with the other.

'I told Basher, Clementine got *really intense* about that soup, okay?'

'Whatever. You can stay in your room if you really want, nobody will care. But I've worked up a plan for the next few days, and we can fill Basher in now.'

'I just want to point out again,' said Sophie, who was trailing along behind them, 'that you are an adult who is being adulted by a teenager. And it's not even me. Claire, you're like thirty.'

This Claire did not repeat, although it did remind her of something she'd wanted to ask about.

'Weird question maybe, but how old is your dad, Alex?'

'Oh. Hmm.' Alex stopped walking to think. 'I want to saaaaay... forty-two? Forty-three? Somewhere around there, anyway. Why?'

'Well, it's a big age gap between him and the others. I thought it might be, you know, relevant if it turned out he was, er, adopted or something like that.'

'Oh, it's far more standard kitchen sink than that. Granny and Grandad got married young, and Granny was eighteen and pregnant. Gasp! Unthinkable!' Here Alex feigned a look of horror. 'Then there was a break for about a decade while they all grew up a bit, and Grandad got a stable job and a decent income and all that lark. And between you and me, I don't think Granny was keen on having another baby any time soon, either. She doesn't like to talk about it – it's not very picture-perfect-family-values of her. But yeah, after Dad it goes Aunt F, Uncle B and poor old Tris on the end. He's properly the baby. Mothered and smothered. So, interesting thought, but no. Dad's meanness is all natural.'

Alex pulled Claire along again, swung round some more corners and pushed her into what turned out to be Basher's room. Basher was looking fretfully through his bag.

'Hey, Uncle B,' said Alex. 'We should probably leave tomorrow, huh?'

Basher sat back on his knees and shoved his hands into their resting position in the front pocket of his hoodie. 'Yes, I agree,' he said. 'We should get out of Mum and Dad's hair while they arrange the funeral. The others are probably shoving off, too. We can drop Claire at the station on our way.'

'And Sophie,' said Alex. 'And no. They are coming with us, obviously.'

'Oh, *obviously*.'

'Well? We have a sofa.'

'Ohmigod! What about the investigation, though?' said Soph, immediately on the verge of being outraged and lining up the ammunition needed to fight this particular battle a second time.

'What do you mean? This *is* the investigation,' Alex replied.

'Now I am also confused,' said Claire. 'Don't we have to stay in the village and uncover all the clues?'

The pitying silence with which Alex met this statement was one of the most humiliating things Claire had ever experienced. 'God,' they said, after a moment. 'No wonder you lot totally failed at solving any global problems, cursing my generation to save the world. *Obviously* we won't stay here. There is no phone signal, internet, or even any actual people. There are no clues. What kind of murder-solving outfit do you think this is? How am I going to clear my family's good name, and be the star of a limited-series documentary, if we don't go about this the right way?'

Claire wondered if Alex was taking this as seriously as Basher thought they were.

'There are some clues,' said Claire sulkily.

'Well,' said Basher, 'I must agree with Alex. Assuming there was a crime – and, by the way, I have to say again that we only have the faintest second-hand suggestion of *financial* crime – the majority of witnesses aren't based here, and since we have no idea where the actual crime scene might be, the chance of uncovering physical evidence is very slim. And, as noted, the resources here are... poor. They'd be poor even with any added official police resources.'

Basher started ticking off things on his fingers, getting quietly excited, despite himself. 'You work it like a cold case, right? The coldest, technically. Establish a timeline, establish persons present, interview witnesses, identify potential corroborating evidence... Identifying the victim would be favourite, of course, but we're coming at that arse-backwards by working out who it is *not*.'

'But look,' Sophie continued, gamely trying to be helpful, 'we still have loads of gaps. Like, what about the entertainment? We haven't even thought about the tragic a cappella group yet. That's like... half a dozen potential victims?'

There was silence after Claire relayed this, as everyone thought about how the whole thing might be more hard work than they'd anticipated.

'But they sound like they'll be pretty easy to track down,' said Claire. 'I'll... er... I'll call them, if you like?' She found she was anxious to contribute more practical help to the operation. Also she had noticed that when Basher was thinking of practical things and steps and the progress of the investigation, he got excited and forgot that his official position was still anti-investigation. He had, for example, ceased to object about Claire and Sophie staying with him and Alex.

'Right, okay, so what we do is,' said Alex, ignoring Claire and stabbing the air with their unlit cigarette, 'we go back to Brighton and talk to Sami, right? Then we go up to London to Claire's and talk to Tris and that accountant guy. And if there's time we also go to Camden.'

'Camden sucks,' said Claire automatically, at the same time as Basher said, 'Camden is awful' and Soph said, 'Camden is fucking great.' Claire met Basher's eyes and they smiled at one another. This pleased her, in the way a child is pleased when they do something to gain adult approval.

Alex waved their hands in the air, batting away this millennial nonsense. 'Sure, fine. And then we put together everything we know and come back for Nana's funeral, where we will be able to—'

'Do a round-up and confront the killer?' finished Claire.

'*No*, Claire,' said Sophie.

'Jesus, Claire, it's a funeral,' said Basher.

'It's what Nana would have wanted,' said Alex, with blank-faced solemnity. 'But nah, I was going to say "poke around the house and grounds again".'

'But shouldn't we interview your family as well, though?' asked Claire. 'They're all suspects!'

'No, no way,' said Basher. 'I'm vetoing that, at least until after the funeral, and at least until you've actually proven that someone is missing. Come on. I'm agreeing you can come to Brighton with us, so compromise with me here.'

'Okay, I suppose that makes sense,' Claire replied, after considering all the angles. Mostly she was keen to leave the house, and the watchful, baleful eye of Clementine.

'I'm on board,' Sophie added.

'Right. I am accepting this plan,' said Basher, 'firstly because the Brighton mainline train can get Claire to London in an hour, if it comes to it. But mostly because it turns out I did not bring my full box of meds, so we do need to get home.'

Alex was concerned. Basher conceded that immediately following your grandmother's death was not an ideal time to discover you had run out of antidepressants.

'I will be fine,' he said. 'I am but mad north-north-west. And I have only missed a day, so nothing to panic about. Probably have a good old despairing and listless stare at the ceiling when I get home, though.'

'I made you that pill organizer and everything,' Alex scolded him.

'It doesn't travel well. It has loads of little dicks on it.'

'Sorry, next time I'll do you one with one of those hamburger cats on, or the physical embodiment of always fucking going on about how you're the last generation to understand why a pencil and a cassette tape are connected. Or whatever it is you people like. Honestly. At what point are you not embarrassed to exist?'

Sophie pointed out that they still needed to properly record a timeline of the events of the suspicious weekend.

'We can do that in the car tomorrow,' said Alex. 'To prevent ourselves from being overheard.' They wiggled their eyebrows conspiratorially, then paused before crashing out of the room again. 'I'm going for a fag,' they said over their shoulder. 'By the way, Uncle

B – Kevin isn't dead, we can definitely cross him off the list.'

Basher sighed and went to stare out of the window. He did that for quite a long time, so eventually Sophie said that Claire should probably go and pack.

PART II

Take nothing on its looks; take everything on evidence. There's no better rule.

Charles Dickens, *Great Expectations*

8

The Time Is Out of Joint

At about 7.45 a.m. the next day, Claire was wedged in the front seat of Basher's car. It was a discreet and battered Peugeot 306 for improved private investigatoring, he had explained, as she'd sat down in it at bang on seven – although Basher had refused to start the car until Claire put her seatbelt on. It'd almost felt like they were escaping like thieves in the night before anyone else noticed. The only person who was there to see them leave was Ted, who was quite sad about it. He'd hooted and waved his cap as if he were seeing off a ship.

Claire viewed most times of day before 11 a.m. as uncivilized, but she had ultimately been glad to leave because, as they'd exited through the kitchen door, she'd come face-to-face with several brace of dead pheasants hanging on a nail on the wall outside. Their eyes were closed and they could almost have been asleep, except that they were strung together by their necks, which lolled uselessly. Some of them – the hens – were speckled brown, but the males had bright green heads and fussy white collars, and long striped tail feathers.

Their features were so soft and lovely, but they looked cold and wet, and Claire had fought an impulse to stroke them and warm them up. Hugh had bragged the day before about how he'd hit, just, loads. Beaten his PB. The chaps had all been really impressed. Then Claire had imagined Clementine gutting, plucking and cooking them, and had scrabbled quickly across the yard.

There was a tacit understanding that none of the living people in the car was really a morning person, and they were not going to make moves towards conversation for a while. Claire spent some time groggily considering The Case. At some point she had slotted in the ominous capital letters, but wasn't sure when. She started scribbling things down on the crumpled bits of paper she found at the bottom of her rucksack: empty Virgin Media envelopes, bus tickets, old napkins in various colours.

Now, in the light of day, things weren't making much more sense than they had the night before. And unfortunately Soph *was* a morning person – and a midday, evening and midnight person – so she was very bored during the drive and kept interrupting Claire's investigative thoughts. She sat behind Claire sighing, huffing and tutting, as well as intermittently humming the same mis-remembered snatch of 'Wannabe' by The Spice Girls. It was this last bit that finally made Claire snap after forty-five minutes.

'You're getting the words wrong! Fucking hell, shut up,' she bawled suddenly, making Basher start. 'Why would it be "Ham your shoddy clown and wipe it up and down"? *Why?*'

'Ohmigod, what is wrong with you this morning? I thought you'd be happy to get out of that house,' said Sophie, pleased to have caused a reaction at last.

They were now barrelling into the New Forest, and although this morning was another cold one, it was bright and brittle and cloud-free. Claire's head rattled uncomfortably against the window and it was making her feel sick, but it was the only angle where the sun didn't get her in the eyes. She was feeling sorry for herself and overwhelmed.

Once, in a spirit of short-lived culinary experimentation that had included attempts to make her own sourdough bread, Claire had tried out baked stuffed apples. When she had pulled the little treasures from the oven, she had been appalled by their appearance, simultaneously wrinkled and wizened, but also horribly full on the insides and oozing out of hitherto unknown orifices. She'd been so put off that she binned the tray and had eaten a whole thing of Mr Kipling mini-pies instead.

Right now, her head felt like one of those apples. It was so full of facts and contradictions and awful things that had happened over the last couple of days that she thought grey matter was going to start leaking out of her ears. She explained this, because she was quite pleased with the metaphor, but it only made Alex and Sophie laugh at her. Basher, who was whistling through his teeth and tapping the steering wheel, said that baked apples are actually quite easy to make, and she must have got the recipe wrong somehow.

'Look, there's a garage coming up in a minute,' he said, relenting at Claire's forlorn expression. 'We can take a break for coffee and terrible pastries. And Topic bars.'

'Why Topic bars?'

'When I used to go anywhere with Nana and Papa – my grandad, the nibling's great-grandad—'

'He died before I was born,' said Alex, who was occupying the two seats in the back that Soph wasn't, by spreading out: a) most of their body; and b) a huge canvas tote bag and the contents thereof, which were many, varied and confusing. They were working on a different embroidery hoop today. It was an image of Baby Yoda, but as if he were a saint on a Catholic votive candle.

'Papa would stop at a garage or whatever and go in to pay for the petrol and get chocolate bars. I hate Topics, but they're Nana's favourite, and I'd sit in the car with her and chant, *'Pick Topic pick Topic pick Topic'* over and over again. I just liked saying the words.'

Basher smiled as they pulled into a standard-issue Shell garage. Claire noticed that Basher and Alex both had red eyes today.

They piled out of the car and inhaled the weird, drill-up-your-nose smell of the forecourt. Claire and Sophie nodded hello at a ghost in oily overalls who was hanging around the pumps, and followed Alex (who was dressing down today, in bootcut jeans and a crisp white T, but under the same signature, crackling black hell-coat) into the shop to load up on supplies. Claire was pleased with her haul:

Item: *tea, one large, grim cardboard cup of*
Item: *saus. roll, two, grey*
Item: *peperami, one, impulse purchase*
Item: *cheese-and-onion crisps, sharing-size bag of*
Item: *sunglasses, one pair, round, silver-framed*

The actual sunshade bit on the lenses of that last item was so graduated that it might as well have been transparent, but needs must when the devil pisses sunshine into your eyeholes.

After some consideration of her bank balance, Claire also got twenty Marlboro Lite and a sharing bag of Starburst. They sat down at a plastic table around the corner to break their fast in style. Basher joined them and accepted a Starbust with the shy smile that Claire was growing to recognize.

She put on her sunglasses.

'You look like a Minion,' said Sophie immediately.

'*You* look like a Minion,' said Claire.

'Ohmigod, I do not, weirdo. I look like a rock star who died tragically before her time,' said Sophie. 'As in, pre-rock star. I definitely would have been a rock star if I'd have had the chance.'

There, variously bickering, flicking fag ash around, collecting sweet wrappers on the table in drifts, yelling, nearly spilling tea on the laptop and insisting on making pen-and-paper notes as well, because it just felt better, they established their timeline.

First thing on the Monday after the party, a truckload of office workers from a nationwide pasta shipping company had turned up, so the timeframe for the murder was quite tight. The most exact timings they had could be locked in by the time-stamps on photos Alex had on their phone. They also knew what times to place people at meals (before they scattered off the timeline again, like so many inconvenient cockroaches into unknown areas under the bath) since Clementine had strict and unwavering deadlines. Breakfast was on the table at 8.30 a.m., lunch at 1 p.m. and dinner at 6.30 in the evening. But apart from that, it was mostly guesswork, without anyone else to corroborate it. Which was, Claire supposed, the point of going to find other people to corroborate it.

Eventually they came up with a serviceable, if messy, list of key events:

Friday 25 October

Clementine, Hugh, Nana assumed all to be at the house. Also assumed Mattie arrived at 10 a.m., via bike, as usual. Monty and Tris reported to have arrived 'about half twelve' with Michael, in Monty's car.

4.17 p.m.	*Alex and Tuppence arrive, also by car*
5 p.m.	*Mattie leaves to go home after work*
6.40–7 p.m.-ish	*Figgy and Kevin arrive by car*
9.01 p.m.	*Basher and Sami arrive, also by car*
1 or 2 a.m.	*Monty, Tris and Michael still up working – heard arguing*

Saturday the 26th

9 a.m.-ish	*Basher explains he quit his job. Breakfast is ruined.*
10 a.m.	*Mattie arrives (dropped off by Alf)*
10.04 a.m.	*Alex gets a lift to the village with Alf*
2 p.m.-ish	*Clementine warns off Kevin*
2.30 p.m.	*Michael asks to go somewhere he can make a phone call*
3.45 p.m.-ish	*Figgy and Kevin argue*
6.30–8.30 p.m.-ish	*Most disastrous birthday dinner in history. Sunday party with wider family guests is cancelled.*

Sunday the 27th

8 a.m.	*Hugh and Tris out on a shoot all day*
10 a.m.	*Mattie doesn't come to work*
1.30 p.m.-ish	*Alex leaves with Basher and Sami*

Monday the 28th

| 8.30 a.m. | *TOI Food Inc. corporate retreat (3 days)* |

Claire cast a critical eye over the list. She'd wanted them to note down more detail, like what was eaten by everyone at every meal, because she had learned from every book or TV murder mystery that this could be crucial information. 'Say that at dinner one night you'd had, like, a really hot sauce,' she pointed out. 'That could have concealed the taste of poison.'

'Ye-e-e-s, probably it could. Although it could not, I fear, have concealed the symptoms of being poisoned,' said Basher. 'They're usually too noisy. Also, we did not have anything with a really hot sauce.'

'Yeah, well. The point is you *might* have had.'

Soph was also looking at the list, and had more pressing concerns.

'*Grave* concerns?' asked Alex, wiggling their brows again (evidently their go-to punchline for a joke).

'That is very insensitive,' said Soph. She yawned lazily, which Claire was almost 100 per cent sure was an affectation, since Sophie did not get tired or need to breathe. 'Tell them I said that coldly.'

'You do everything coldly,' replied Claire. Alex snickered. Nevertheless, Sophie asked them to fill in, in more detail, what they had seen *after* the fateful dinner on Saturday night, since previously they had been derailed by talking about family dysfunction and going to the pub. The answer was: not much.

'I went and had a cup of tea with Sami and Nana, in Nana's room,' said Basher. 'We had a bit of the cake, as well. Nana fell asleep around half ten, and Sami and I both went back to our rooms after that. Sami was in the same room as you were, facing the garden, so she might have heard something.'

'I was hanging out with Mum in the kitchen for a bit. I *think* Granny and Grandad were there too – no, actually, Grandad was watching football or rugby or something,' said Alex. 'Then, after a bit, I went up to my room. I was having a secret spliff, tee-emm, out of the window and I heard Granny having a go at Uncle T for ruining his suit – he got it all covered in mud. So that's how I know he fell over. But I don't know what time that was. Sorry.'

'It's really annoying that you two left so early on Sunday, because you didn't see Hugh and Tristan come back from their shoot, and you didn't see loads of people leave. Sunday is *very* thin. In fact...' Claire narrowed her eyes. 'I don't think you saw any of our potential victims leave at all.'

Basher pulled the analogue paper list towards him, while Sophie leaned over to look at Alex's screen. Basher frowned. 'No, you're right. There are a lot of '-ish' times as well.'

'When was the last time you saw Mattie?' Claire asked. 'You didn't see her leave on Saturday, and she didn't come in on Sunday?'

'No. Alex?' asked Basher.

Alex shook their head. 'I saw her on Saturday when she arrived, but not when she left.'

'And does she normally work at weekends?'

'Yes,' said Basher. 'Weekends are busier than weekdays for events, right? Mattie's normal days off are Monday and Tuesday. That weekend, I think she didn't strictly need to be there; she was just in the office doing paper-work and admin.'

'We know what happens to people who go in there,' said Sophie darkly.

'So,' said Claire slowly, immensely pleased because she was pretty sure she was forming a full piece of useful data in real time, 'even if something happened to Mattie that weekend, you wouldn't have thought it was weird if—'

'If nobody in the family heard from Mattie on Monday or Tuesday,' finished Basher. 'It gives you nearly two full days of grace, if you'd murdered her.'

'But the most sus person there, based on circumstantial evidence, is Grandad,' said Alex, 'and he was out at the shoot all day Sunday, so he couldn't have been burying a body or anything.'

'Ahh,' said Soph, 'but was he? You two weren't at the shoot cos you'd left by the time he and Tris supposedly came back, and you haven't checked with anyone else who was at this supposed shoot to confirm Hugh's alibi. Who's to say? We have reason to believe the body was hidden in the priest-hole at some point. Maybe that's why it was stashed there – playing for time until the murderer could bury it secretly.'

Basher, as seemed to happen whenever he did some investigative work, was warming up to it and putting himself in a good mood. This was the case even if, or possibly especially because, he was investigating his own family.

'We know Kevin spirited himself away sometime between Saturday night and Sunday breakfast,' he went on. 'That's a massive window. Say, ten hours.'

'Yes, *but*, Uncle B, we already ruled out Kevin. At what point mustn't we definitively let Kevin go? It sounds like Kevin has let Kevin go even. And, soon, Aunt F should, as well.'

Michael the accountant could not clearly be placed leaving, either. In fact he was something of an enigma all round. If nothing else, one's accountant seemed like quite a weird choice of house-guest for your nan's birthday. Apparently he had been a somewhat unexpected one.

Monty and Tristan, Basher explained, had phoned with only a couple of hours' notice to say that they were bringing Michael down, because they needed him for the urgent work they were handling that weekend. Alex specifically remembered Clementine's potato-based concerns around the dinner. Apart from the meals, the three had spent most of their time either in the office or in Tristan's room working – which was where Basher heard them arguing on the Friday night when he got up for a slash.

Basher described Michael as taller and better-looking than Monty, which was an extra source of tension, but he seemed more devoted to good accountancy than anything else, with nothing in his life except work. It, or things related to it, were the only things he talked about.

'I expect,' said Basher, 'that Michael has loads of people mooning after him all the time, competing to somehow be the last one in the office working late with him, but he doesn't even notice because they're not quarterly figures.'

Alex produced a picture with Michael in the background. He was indeed a tall and very good-looking Black man, with a large, strong jaw, a shaved head and excellent shoulders. His suit was clearly less expensive than the ones Monty wore, but was doing more for him, which did seem like the sort of thing Monty would dislike.

'It was really late – or, well, early,' said Basher, 'and they were still at it in Tris's room, but arguing, not working. But the weird thing was they were arguing about breakfast.'

'Breakfast?'

'Yeah. I couldn't make it out exactly and I didn't think much of it at the time, but I definitely remember thinking it was strange. I could hear Tris doing his wheedling "Oh, come on, mate" voice, and Monty doing his more normal angry bellend voice – sorry, Alex.'

Alex made an 'eh' noise and wobbled their hand in the air.

'And then I heard Michael say something about breakfast. "I'm serious", he said, about… sausage? I wish I could remember. I suppose I should have paid more attention, but I had my own things to deal with. I just assumed it was business stuff about one of their clients, I suppose. Or that Michael really was that serious about hollandaise.'

That added more weight to the idea that some financial irregularities had been discovered. Claire pointed out the time on Saturday when Michael asked to go somewhere to make a phone call. 'Was that when Kevin drove him to the